THE BROKEN DAUGHTER

THE LOST DAUGHTERS TRILOGY BOOK TWO

VIOLA TEMPEST

The Broken Daughter
The Lost Daughters Trilogy Book Two

Website: www.violatempest.com

Cover Design by Ann Fleur Art

The Broken Daughter

THE LOST DAUGHTERS TRILOGY BOOK TWO

VIOLA TEMPEST

KINGDOM OF PEACE
BAOSHU KINGDOM
SHENHUA KINGDOM

ORPHANAGE
N
W
E
S
JINU KINGDOM
NAJAE ISLAND

CONTENTS

CHAPTER ONE

THE RIGID WINTERS AND OPACITY OF THIS TOWN WERE something a person could *never* escape from. It transferred from one person to the next, killing the smallest speck of light and hope within a soul.

There she was, standing at a distance, radiating light with all her glory and prestige, looking elegant as one could ever be while surrounded by an army of soldiers.

"Xiuying?" Xiaofan heard herself say. "The queen?" she questioned herself. "How?" she muttered. The sister her parents had abandoned was now a queen?

She failed to understand what had happened as she peeked from the tiny window of her room, hearing chants of people praising the queen.

The town hadn't had a visitor for ages, or ever since Xiaofan was sent here, and what were the odds? The only time the town ever got a visitor, and it turned out to be her long-lost sister?

She forced herself to understand that this was just a sheer coincidence and had *nothing* to do with her very existence, and she climbed under her sheets and let all the memories sink in. The child who was once loved, admired, and cherished in a wealthy kingdom, served by hundreds of servants, maids, and soldiers, was now taking shelter at an orphanage that had nothing to offer but dismay, oppression, and dampness.

Xiaofan now found herself deprived of everything that her parents had once promised her. She was the second daughter of Qianfan and Daiyu, the king and queen of Jinu. Parents who had once abandoned their firstborn daughter in spite of not having a son, accepted Xiaofan, celebrated her, and gave her all the love that a child deserved. The early years of her childhood were spent in pure bliss, admired by her father, treasured by her mother, and respected by the entire kingdom.

She was the most respected in political and educational trials. From a very young age, she had a better understanding of complex matters than those around her, her comprehension levels above and beyond those of the local adults. She was proud, and rightfully so. She had *everything*—status, wealth, power, and rank. Though these things made it difficult for her to make friends her own age.

She never got along with other girls her age; she always thought they were below her, and she was superior to them. The love and power surrounding her daily life had taken over her mind and soul.

However, the oblivious child in her didn't know that pride wasn't enough, and *her* pride eventually fell. She saw her future in the kingdom among rulers, but her father had other plans for her, and her mother never questioned his decisions.

It had been eleven years since she was sent here, and she still remembered the warmth of her mother's love, her voice, and her touch of affection. She still remembered the conversations about politics with her father, their friendly chess matches, and him telling her how much she reminded him of his younger self. The memories were still embedded in her heart and mind, especially the harsh ones and the series of events that led her here.

She tried to turn a deaf ear to the chants coming from outside and closed her eyes to sleep, allowing all the events to reoccur in her mind.

ELEVEN YEARS AGO...

. . .

On a balmy morning during the rich season of spring, eight-year-old Xiaofan woke up in her enormous room that was right next to her parents' room. The room had been painted a shade of lavender and decorated with painted portraits of her family. She had a large wooden desk in the corner that had every quality of paper and ink that ever existed. It was her *favorite* part of the room as she *loved* creating stories.

Next to the desk was a shelf that had books with all her writings and also some works by famous literature writers. Her space was *always* lit up with oil lamps and scented candles, the fragrance of vanilla essence constantly lingering in the air.

She managed to get out of bed, her sheets smoother than silk and her pillows soft like clouds. Her bedroom had two huge windows on two different walls—one showed her the view of the entire castle, and the other allowed her to look over her kingdom. She walked across her room and stood in front of the window that allowed her to see her kingdom and the tiny homes that people lived in.

How do they live in such tiny homes? she would often think to herself.

As much pride as she had, she *did* try to stay humble. She was lucky to be here, she knew that. She was fortunate to have the wisdom to understand worldly matters, and she made a vow to herself to work hard so she could help the people of her kingdom and raise their living standards.

The door to her room suddenly pushed open,

pulling her out of her thoughts. It was one of her maids.

"The queen has birthed a son," the maid revealed. "Congratulations, you have a baby brother."

Xiaofan turned with her answer. "Prepare my dress. I shall go see him."

The maid paused before replying, "The king *forbids* anyone from seeing the queen and the newborn for the next three days, and he expects you to understand."

Xiaofan took a step back. *Why? Why would he forbid me from seeing my own brother?* She failed to understand the decree, but she could do little to argue against her father's orders.

Three days went by, and Xiaofan was excited to finally meet her new baby brother. She ordered her maid to bring her the best dresses that she had. She shook her head and smiled as she left, only to return with ten different options for her. Xiaofan chose one and started to get ready.

What will it be like to have a sibling? she thought to herself as she combed her long locks, oblivious to the fact that she already had a sibling.

Xiaofan tied her hair back and took a look in the mirror. Her fair face with rosy pink cheeks was glowing, and her hair tied back looked elegant. She'd made an *excellent* choice with her dress, choosing to wear a lilac dress with ruffled sleeves. She looked divine, like a princess should.

"Perfect," she complimented herself and swirled.

She then left her room, followed by two soldiers and three maids who accompanied her everywhere.

Her parents' room was at the end of the royal corridor. It was right next to *her* room, but it took at least five minutes to walk there, and Xiaofan *never* left her room without her army of soldiers and maids, even if it *was* for just five minutes.

The maids knocked on the door to the king and queen's room and announced Xiaofan's presence. They allowed her to enter, and when she stepped in, she saw a small baby boy wrapped in a dark blue blanket that had dragon patterns embroidered on it. Daiyu was holding him close to her while Qianfan was sitting right next to her. Xiaofan came running in to see her brother, but she was not allowed to touch him.

"Stop right there!" Qianfan yelled as he saw Xiaofan leaning in to hold the boy. "Are your hands clean?" he questioned. "We cannot take *any* chances with the newborn."

"Yes, Father, they are," Xiaofan whispered.

"You can just watch him from afar," Qianfan declared, now standing up on his feet and looking down over the boy.

"Honey, give it some time. You will get a lot of time to spend with your brother," Daiyu whispered in a low voice with her eyes still on the boy. She didn't even look at Xiaofan for a second.

"Okay," Xiaofan murmured.

"Now that you have seen the newborn, you should head back to your room," Qianfan ordered.

"Yes, my dear. The ball is tonight, and there are still so many things to do in preparation," Daiyu added.

"Can I come to the ball, Mother?" Xiaofan asked, looking up at her mother with glowing eyes.

"Yes, of course, but for now, you need to get going."

Xiaofan shook her head, indicating that she understood, but her inner monologue was failing to understand why Qianfan and Daiyu were treating her differently than before. She slowly left the room, and her army escorted her back to her own room.

She marched in and slammed the door shut behind her. Something had changed; she could feel it in her bones and in the air. She felt like her place was being taken. She was being *replaced* by someone better, even if that someone was just an infant. The anger in her was something that she had inherited from her father, and *that* was what channeled her magical power the most. She had control over wind and fire, and she was being taught by the wise wizard of the castle how to control them.

After hours of envying her new baby brother, Xiaofan decided to get ready for the ball. The festivities had begun, and the castle looked like a completely different place. It was decorated from one corner to another with flowers and silk drapes, and guests were arriving with presents and treats.

Xiaofan could see all the glory from her room. This was something that she had never experienced, she had *never* seen something being celebrated to such transcendent extents at the castle.

The maids knocked and entered her room, bringing a gown with them that was specifically made for her and sent by her mother. The dress was a pastel purple silk dress with long bell sleeves and traditional flowers embroidered onto it with jewels.

"The queen has requested that you wear this," the head maid said, and Xiaofan nodded as a sign of assurance.

Xiaofan was a little relieved after receiving the dress. "She didn't forget about me," she muttered to herself and started to get ready for the ball.

As much as Xiaofan was fond of the perks of being a royal, she hated gatherings; she hated meeting people and pretending to be nice to them. A royal ball was the *last* event that she looked forward to, and this time, she was already annoyed. In spite of the newborn, her mood swings were already unpredictable, and they would only get worse during the celebration.

The ball had begun, and the main hall was filled with royal families from all around the country. Xiaofan arrived an hour late and greeted everyone with smiles and hugs.

Oh, the misery, she thought every time she had to sweet talk another elderly person.

After twenty minutes, the guards announced the arrival of the king, queen, and the prince. They walked in with all the grandeur of a happy and powerful royal family. Daiyu was holding the newborn, and Qianfan walked by her side. He was prouder than he had ever been his entire life. They came upfront while everyone showered them with flowers.

"After years and years of waiting, we have finally been blessed with an heir, a prince. A boy who is going to continue our legacy, just like I did, just like my father did, and just like our ancestors did. Today is a blessed day that needs to be celebrated with all our hearts," Qianfan announced in a loud, strong, and firm voice, silencing the crowd before them. "We name him Jinhai, for he is the golden sea that is going to bring in enlightenment."

Qianfan then took the magical stone to mark Jinhai's wrist as per tradition. The packed hall started to chant, "Long live Prince Jinhai! Long live Prince Jinhai!"

Daiyu broke into happy tears as she watched the scene unfold before her while Qianfan held onto her hand tightly and grinned. Xiaofan watched the events from where she stood above them.

Why am I here and not down there with them? Am I not a part of the family? Questions started to boil in her mind one by one, when suddenly, she heard a whisper.

"It was never like this when you or your sister was born."

Xiaofan paused, and then continued in a low voice, "When I was born?"

"It was a little like this, but *this* is a *lot more.*" One of the maids revealed herself. "But at least you were welcomed. Your elder sister was not."

"What are you saying?" Xiaofan asked as shock and disbelief sparked under her skin. "*I* am the first-born; I don't have a sister."

The maid, who was known as Fang, suddenly realized how big of a mistake she had just made. She tried to take back her words, but it was too late. Xiaofan left the crowded ball and took Fang to her room, where she had no choice but to come clean to Xiaofan. While her parents and their guests were enjoying the ball, eating and drinking their hearts out while they celebrated, the somber truths of the castle and her parents were exposed to Xiaofan inside her room.

Fang told her everything—how Xiuying was born, how she wasn't accepted by Qianfan, how she was abandoned and raised by Mei, her attempted suicide, and her eventual expulsion to an abandoned island to die. Xiaofan just stood there while absorbing all the tales, staring at the kingdom in blissful hysteria from her room's window.

Her heart pounded in her chest as tears started to roll down her cheeks.

"Please, don't tell *anyone* that you heard this from me. They will incarcerate me, just like they imprisoned Mei," Fang pleaded.

"I won't tell anyone, I promise." Xiaofan sobbed. "I would like to be left alone now."

"Are you sure?" Fang asked, and Xiaofan nodded.

As soon as Fang walked out, Xiaofan fell to her

knees, struggling to breathe. "It has all been a lie!" She shook her head but failed to understand. "It has all been a lie!" she screamed again and cried.

How can this be true?

How can they just abandon my sister like that?

Is their love for me even real, or is it all just a lie?

My entire life has been a lie, a false reality.

She could not contain herself any longer. She felt neglect and rage, so she decided to confront the source of all this... her parents. After all, she *was* her father's daughter.

The ball had now ended, and no one noticed that Xiaofan wasn't there.

Without asking for permission, she stomped her way over to her parents' room and slammed open the door, yelling, "Why didn't you ever tell me that I have a sister?"

Her father didn't even look surprised to see her standing there, her face fuming red. Her mother, at least, had the nerve to be a little shocked at her appearance.

"Because it is not important for you to know," Daiyu replied in polite disbelief at Xiaofan's outburst.

"And why is *he* a prince, and I'm not a princess?" Xiaofan pointed over to the newborn and back to herself.

Qianfan walked toward her slowly, his footsteps hitting hard on the floor. He gripped her shoulders tightly, in a way that sent a sharp ache through her joints.

"He is a *he*," Qianfan stated firmly. "*He* is a boy, and *you* are a girl. There's no such thing as a princess. He is superior to you."

Xiaofan stepped back, and the rage she saw in her father today was different... scarier.

"Where is Xiuying?" Xiaofan mumbled as fear took over, and her anger shifted toward despair.

Qianfan tied his hands back, started to walk toward his newborn, and chuckled. "Oh, Xiuying! She's probably dead by now." Xiaofan gasped, but that only made his wicked smile widen. "I sent her away. She *destroyed* our family and your mother." He paused, giving her a long look before he opened his mouth again. "We treated you right, and look how karma repaid us. We have been blessed with a boy *only* because we gave you everything you needed."

Xiaofan couldn't believe the words that she was hearing from her own father's lips. All this time, he hadn't loved her. He had done what he needed to do in order to obtain what he *really* wanted—a son. She meant *nothing* to him. Xiuying had been a victim of his hate, and though Xiaofan thought she was different, clearly, she had been wrong, too. But her father was not content with stopping there.

"If you don't agree with the decisions that I have made, maybe it is time for you to go, too." He scowled at her.

Xiaofan shuddered and took a few steps back. Was the person standing in front of her *really* her father?

The one she played chess with and had conversations with about politics? Her eyes were red with tears.

Daiyu interrupted at that moment, sensing the tension in the room. "Sweetheart, just go to your room. There's nothing for you to worry about or know about. Don't question your father."

Xiaofan stared at her in disbelief. After the lies, the hate, the threats from her own father—her mother would not stand for her, either. She nodded in a shaken state of horror at what her father might do to her. The possibilities were limitless.

She ran toward her room with a broken heart and shattered hope.

CHAPTER
TWO

XIAOFAN COULD NOT STOP SHIVERING WHEN SHE GOT BACK TO her room, her shoulders aching from her father's grip. She felt like someone had crushed her bones, and her soul had left her body. She sat down on her bed with her arms wrapped tightly around herself.

"It'll be fine," she comforted herself, now understanding that she was living in a glass castle that was bound to break by someone she loved the most. The king was only going to be a father for a *boy*. That was loud and clear.

A few days had gone by, and the weather was

changing. The subtle spring had transformed itself into worrisome winters for Xiaofan. She had not seen her parents or heard from them, but she would hear from her maids about their affection toward the newborn. The efforts that they were making to mark his name in the kingdom and its history were great already.

Every day, Qianfan would distribute golden coins and food amongst the underprivileged people of the kingdom to show his gratitude, to show love to his people. But Xiaofan knew now that it's all just a show, an act of pretense to care for everyone in his kingdom.

Rumors and whispers floated around the castle, questioning the presence of Xiaofan. From maids to soldiers, everyone was debating over what Xiaofan's fate would be while she locked herself in her room, isolating from the world and praying that this was all just a horrible nightmare.

Qianfan, on the other hand, was planning to get rid of her.

"Karma has spoken," he told himself. "There's no need to deal with her anymore, especially after she dared talk back to me. How *dare* she?" he whispered to himself.

His mind came up with ways to send her away, but what would he say to Daiyu? How would he convince her to send Xiaofan away, especially after Xiuying? The only person he ever held in high regards after himself was Daiyu. He loved her, but not the girls, even though they were smaller versions of his beloved. How unfortunate was he to not understand the worth of having girls born into his family?

Xiaofan's attitude toward other people had changed. Suddenly, the contentment, the reliance on the kingdom, and the trust in her parents had all vanished into thin air. The experience had somehow made her humble, humble enough to have normal conversations with the maids who looked after her growing up. Humble enough to make her understand the harsh realities of life and how quickly people can change.

This was the first time she didn't feel like she was in control. She felt feeble, yet she understood how the people of the kingdom lived—without any control and under a ruler who worked only for himself. How naïve she was to think that she would be able to help the people of the kingdom out of their mediocre miseries. She, too, was stuck behind the walls of false affection and sheer simulation.

Maybe I deserve this, she thought to herself. *This is what I get when I think I'm above and beyond everyone and everything.* Her thoughts spoke while she admired the tiny homes that she could see from her room's window. All was quiet, all was dark inside her, when all of a sudden, the door to her room swung open, and she was surprised to see her parents walk in.

"Oh, I'm so happy to see you!" Xiaofan gushed and rushed over to hug her mother while Qianfan stood next to her with a dreadful face in silence.

"I am afraid I am here with unsettling news, my

darling," Daiyu muttered as she held onto Xiaofan's hand. "Your father thinks it's best that you go to training school, a place where you can learn how to behave like a royal and gain better control over your power."

"And your mother agrees," Qianfan added. "We both think it'll be best for you to move away from here. All the arrangements have been made, and you will leave today."

Xiaofan's heart sank deep into the depths of dismissal.

What's happening? They're choosing the newborn over me, and I'm going to end up like Xiuying.

"No!" she shouted and took two steps back. "No! This is my home. I am *not* going anywhere! Don't send me away," she pleaded, trying to get Daiyu to understand. To stand up for her.

"Sweetheart, this is only temporary; you will come back. But for now, you will have to go. This is what's best for you," Daiyu casually responded, barely meeting her daughter's teary gaze.

"You leave in two hours," Qianfan stated firmly. "Pack your things, everything you need, and *don't* leave anything behind," he added with a smile creeping onto his face that only showed how his plan was working out.

"This is goodbye, Xiaofan, but only for a little while," Daiyu told her. She hugged her daughter quickly and left the room, leaving Xiaofan behind in a state of hysteria.

"This is goodbye... forever," Qianfan hissed after Daiyu was gone. "You are going to pay for the rest of your life for questioning me." And then he left the room without any regret.

Xiaofan broke down completely once she was left alone once again. "Why? Why? Why?!" she cried out. "I'm sorry. Let me stay! Let me stay!" she screamed, but all her cries fell on deaf ears. There wasn't a single person in sight who would stand up for her against Qianfan.

The maids started packing her things, putting them all in wooden crates. In a matter of minutes, her room was no longer her home. It felt empty, just like her soul. She quietly sat in the corner, watching all the boxes get carried out by the soldiers.

"It's time to leave," Fang whispered in a low voice. "I'm sorry. I wish I could help you, but my hands are tied."

Xiaofan stood up with no expression on her face and started to walk out of the room. She was escorted to the grand castle door and was told to wait. After a while, Qianfan appeared.

"Farewell!" He waved with a laugh. "I'm sure you wish that you stayed within your given limits because that's where tiny dolls like you belong. The consequences of questioning me are going to weigh over your little wish of being treated equally to your brother." He paused, and then added, "Oh, apologies. Not your brother—the prince."

Xiaofan stood there in silence. She didn't reply; she

didn't cry; she didn't plead to let her stay. She just accepted her fate, and after a while, the royal carriage took her to the harbor, and she boarded the ship without any hesitation.

AFTER A JOURNEY OF ABOUT TWO DAYS, FEELING AND SEEING all the blues, Xiaofan reached a small town. The steps ahead were only going to take her further away from her past self. She stood up straight on the deck, her body stiff, and she looked over at the wooden boxes that contained her life, which were now being transported from the ship to a black carriage. She turned around and saw the flag of her kingdom waving against the strong winds, the colors prominent over the background of dark gray clouds. This was probably the last time she would experience something that made her belong to royalty. This was probably the last time her eyes would look at the flag that once represented her home.

It was time to leave and board the carriage. She walked down the steps to the wooden harbor that looked like it would sink into the sea any minute. She sat inside the carriage, and it started to move toward a dark alley. The roads were not built properly, and the wheels of the carriage kept hitting against the loose rocks. There were no lights or lamps in the streets, there was an unbearable stench that felt like it was coming from a rotten corpse, and the hair-raising vibes and eerie atmosphere were making her fear what was ahead.

After an hour of traveling on a pathway that felt like it was never going to end, they reached a building that was in the middle of nowhere. And surrounded by a brick wall was a two-story cottage that was painted gray with black windows, and a chimney that had smoke billowing out of it. There was no greenery in sight, the grass had turned brown, and the trees were barren with dark black crows sitting on them.

Xiaofan stepped out, and her heart started to beat faster and faster with every second. She looked around and saw a few single-story shops around the borders of the cottage with rotten fruits and vegetables on display.

The gates opened, and she walked in, the soldiers carrying the wooden boxes behind her. The maid rang the doorbell, and the back door opened. A tall, stocky woman stepped out, standing straight. She was dressed in a black gown, her dark hair was tied in a braid, and she had a round face with tiny eyes that were covered by the glasses she was wearing.

"Look at this! The *princess* is here," she mocked in a sarcastic tone. "Come in, come in!" she whispered, and Xiaofan stepped in the house, taking small steps. The soldiers were told to bring the boxes into her room upstairs.

The cottage was an orphanage for young girls who had no one to look after them, all living under one roof. The wooden floor creaked with every step

Xiaofan took. There were paintings of the founders hanging on each of the gray walls, the furniture was old and rusty, a huge wooden staircase led to the upper floor, and there were a few oil lamps lit up that looked like they were about to run out of juice.

Xiaofan was numb. At this point, she didn't just blame her father. She blamed herself for letting her anger cloud her mind, for letting pride take over her. Karma was performing an act of revenge, and she's its latest victim. She stood silent by the staircase as the soldiers placed all her things inside, and then they left without saying a single word to Xiaofan, leaving her there all alone with the woman wearing glasses.

"So, you are the princess whom Qianfan got rid of," she commented, and then continued in a harsh tone, "I am Liling, the headmistress of this orphanage. Now that you are here, you will have to live by *our* rules—eat what we eat, wear what the other girls wear, and have the same lifestyle as every other orphan girl here." She paused, studying Xiaofan's small form dressed in fine clothing made with royal fabrics and jewels. She scowled before continuing, "Forget about the castle because you are *never* going back there. I only agreed to keep you here because the king has offered me a generous donation. Now off you go! The first room on the left upstairs is yours."

Xiaofan bowed and silently went to find her room.

She could hear every step she took; the silence in this place was deafening. The door squeaked as she forced it open. It was a tiny room with simple gray painted walls, a small window with no curtains, and a single bed with plain white sheets and one blanket. The place was not only dark, but it was cold as well. It made her feel like she was being buried alive, her new home suffocating her.

She entered the room and closed the door behind her. The tiny room was filled with all the wooden boxes that contained her life. She sat down on the bed, took a deep breath, and started to sob without even realizing that her eyes were pouring tears. She curled up under the blanket with her arms and knees folded to her chest, questioning her very existence, questioning her life ahead, her future. She felt lonely; she had no one.

A heavy knock on her room's door disturbed her silence, and she sprung up, startled with dried tears on her face and an aching body. She struggled to get out of bed, but somehow managed to reach the door and open it up... finding herself face-to-face with a little girl her age.

"Hey," the girl said in a sweet and gentle tone. She was dressed in a long off-white gown that had a little touch of black embroidery around the neckline. She had a thin face with round eyes and long dark brown hair.

"Hi," Xiaofan responded, her voice a choked croak from all her tears.

"Can I come in?" the girl asked.

"Sure." Xiaofan opened the door wider.

"Are you okay?" the girl asked, stepping inside. "We all heard you crying."

"I'm okay," Xiaofan answered awkwardly, avoiding the girl's eyes. But then something struck her. "We?" she asked.

"Yes, all the girls—they're worried about you. We look out for each other here, and you are one of us now," the girl replied, sitting on the corner of Xiaofan's bed.

Xiaofan hesitated. "That's very thoughtful, but I'm okay." She'd never made friends and never interacted with children her age before, especially when she was at the castle, and now when they were trying to bring forward a hand of friendship, a hand of support, she hesitated.

"Alright." The girl stood up. "I understand that you are overwhelmed right now, but we are here if you want some company." The girl smiled and moved to leave, but she stopped in the doorway. "Oh, and my name is Fia."

"Xiaofan," Xiaofan mumbled, and Fia nodded and left.

Part of her wanted to follow the girl, to have someone—something—to stick to in her time of confusion and despair. But the larger part of her wanted nothing more than to be left alone. So, she closed the door to her room, encasing herself in silent darkness, and she sat down on her bed again.

This place was soaking every tiny bit of hope and

life that she had left in her; darkness was all around her and affecting who she was. The girl who had ambitions, dreams, and hope was now broken, far too gone.

She was sitting alone, gazing at the moonlight shining through the tiny window when a quote that she had recently read crossed her mind.

Things get broken, and sometimes, they get repaired. But in most cases, you realize that no matter what gets damaged, life will always rearrange itself to compensate for your loss, sometimes wonderfully.

She chuckled over the fact that when she'd read it in the comfort of the castle, she believed every word of it. But now she felt like her soul was shattered into miniscule pieces that were impossible to put back together. She was broken in a way that could not be repaired.

Her thoughts were interrupted by a knock on the door... yet again.

Xiaofan stood up, got off the bed to open the door, and saw a group of bright smiles staring back at her.

"Yes?" Xiaofan asked, a bit annoyed.

"We brought you dinner," Fia answered. "And we thought we could all eat together."

Another girl added, "You should join us in Fia's room."

They waited for her to respond. How could she refuse a group of young girls who were only trying to be there for her? How could she tell them that she really didn't need any company? How could she tell them that all she wanted was to remain alone?

"So? Are you joining us?" Fia asked.

Without another second of hesitation, Xiaofan tried to smile. "Yes."

All the girls cheered after hearing her response, and they all ran straight to Fia's room. Xiaofan followed the group after closing her room's door behind her.

Fia's room felt different. She had two oil lamps that made her room bright, and she was an artist. Her room had a lot of colorful paintings on the walls, the colors making her room feel alive and joyful compared to the rest of the orphanage.

"We all usually have dinner together at the dining table in the main hall," Fia said. "But we wanted to make you feel more at home, so we're here." She smiled at Xiaofan just as the others nodded and did much of the same.

Xiaofan didn't know how to respond. "Thank you. I appreciate this, but I don't need it," she murmured.

"Of course, you need it. We all remember our first days, and they were horrible!" another girl, Xiang, added.

They all ate their dinner, and then started to share stories of their lives before the orphanage and how they ended up here. They didn't force Xiaofan to talk or share hers, but they shared their own anyway to make her feel welcomed. They seemed comfortable in telling their tales, Xiaofan noticed. There was no shame, no embarrassment.

Fia shared her story first. Her parents died in a

carriage accident when she was only three years old, and her own relatives refused to take care of her. All they wanted was to get rid of her, so they sent her to this place, and she'd lived here for as long as she could remember. At first, this place was torture, but it got better after she started to make some friends. She was one of the first orphans here, and even from the very beginning, the staff never cared about the well-being of the children. They never invested in them, all their funds and donations used by the headmistress herself. Nothing came easy at this place.

Xiang was next to share her tale. Her mother died while giving birth to her, and her father blamed her for it. He refused to take her in or even see her face, forcing the nurse who helped birthed her to care for her. But after she started her own family, she also sent Xiang away, which was how she ended up here at the age of five. But she did experience love for a short while, even if it couldn't last.

Fia and Xiang were best friends. They had been there for each other ever since they'd met, and they started this tradition of welcoming new girls so that they wouldn't have to go through the same terrible experiences that they had. Xiang had experienced the worst verbal and physical abuse by the headmistress. She made Xiang do all the chores in one day—from cleaning the dishes to washing, drying, *and* folding all the clothes, from mopping the floors to dusting the rusty furniture. Liling made her do everything without any breaks, and at the end of the day, she was exhausted, aching, and had blisters all over her hands.

Liling also considered Xiang to be unlucky, and she made her realize that she was always going to bring bad luck for herself and everyone around her. For every bad thing that happened to Liling or to the orphanage, Xiang was blamed and held accountable, even if it had *nothing* to do with her. It was cruel, unfair, and Xiaofan felt her chest swell with anger at all the stories. The headmistress had been rude enough to *her* when *she* arrived. She couldn't even imagine the tortures that all these girls faced every day at her hands.

The next two girls to speak were sisters, Lanying and Luna. Both of them were very close to one another, sisters who were the best of friends. Their parents left them at the doorstep of this orphanage because they could not afford to feed them. And once again, Xiaofan was reminded of the little homes in her kingdom that she used to watch through her window. Her hopes, her dreams—her promises to help them. The underprivileged people had to give up everything, even their own children.

The sisters' parents left them last year, promising to return, and the sisters still believed that their parents would come back for them one day. But unbeknownst to them, that promise would never come true. Luna was a year older than Lanying, their ages eight and seven. They were both happy most of the time because they were together, even if most days were bad days inside the orphanage.

The rules to earn food were tricky; one mistake, and a child was without it for an entire day. Sometimes they had to share food or even go to sleep hungry. But the sisters made a pact that if one of them didn't get any, they'd always split what they had between the two, so neither of them would ever have to go to sleep without.

The last girl in the group seemed like a loner, not speaking or smiling as much as the others did. Her name was Suki, and she came to the orphanage willingly because her parents got divorced and remarried. Both of them created new happy families of their own, and after sweeping away their past, they swept their first daughter away with it. Neither of them wanted to keep her, and that left her with no other place to go. She came to the orphanage for shelter, food, and maybe a little bit of hope.

The group of girls inspired Xiaofan. All of them had different heartbreaking stories, but they managed to fight through all the odds and put their trust in life. Xiaofan could see it in their eyes, their smiles, and the way they told their stories with courage. This confidence, this humbling togetherness, put Xiaofan at ease. Her chest loosened, and her muscles relaxed. For the first time in days, the tears stayed away. She took a deep breath, and she decided to share her story as well.

She mumbled everything from start to finish,

including how she'd treated people and looked at those who were less privileged than her. She explained what happened to her sister, the birth of her brother, and how her father sent her here to get rid of her. She even told them how she thought this was karma's revenge for how she'd behaved.

"Don't say that!" Suki comforted her. "There's always a plan for us, and things happen for a reason."

"Exactly," Fia agreed.

"And these circumstances are not the best, but at least you have us." Lanying smiled.

"Maybe," Xiaofan murmured.

They all became quiet as she thought about her past, her family, and what was to come. But then the realities of her new life in the orphanage took over. Fia broke the silence and started discussing the details for tomorrow. Chores were assigned to everyone, including Xiaofan, and in order to earn food for the day, she had to make sure that whatever she was assigned was completed with perfection. Xiaofan could think about her family, their betrayal, and her future later. For now, she needed to survive this place.

CHAPTER THREE

The first morning at the orphanage felt like a living nightmare. Xiaofan woke up in a room that felt like a prison cell. She got out of bed, and shivers passed down her spine. And as her feet touched the cold marble floor, she gathered herself and went to wash up, only to pull her hands back when the freezing cold water touched her. There was no source of heat inside the orphanage, and the fireplace was only lit when the headmistress wanted to sit beside it, never allowing any of the girls to come near her.

Xiaofan's chore today was to clean all the bathrooms—all *eight* of them. This particular chore was supposed to be the toughest, and everyone knew that Liling was trying to torture her on purpose. But Xiaofan refused to back down from the challenge. She got dressed in the white gown that had been given to her—the same one that every girl was given to show that they belong to the orphanage—and walked down the stairs to find Liling standing at the base.

"Our tiny princess will be cleaning all the bathrooms today. Your tiny little hands are going to get all dirty!" She laughed while handing over a bucket of soapy water and a mop. "Get started if you want to save yourself from hunger. And make sure *everything* is sparkling clean. I will make you do it all over again if I see even a single speck of dirt."

Xiaofan silently took the cleaning supplies and nodded. She found herself inside the first bathroom, and the stench was making it hard to breathe. One look at the grime settled into every nook and cranny, and her tenacity crumbled.

"I can't do this. I can't do this," she repeated to herself, staring at the dirty walls and muddy floor. Never before had she had to clean. Never before had she thought she would. But now her survival banked on her ability to do it properly.

"Why?" she choked on a rising sob.

She sat outside the door and tried to calm herself as she realized how poorly she'd treated her maids at the castle. She had insulted them, taunted them, and now she was doing what they did every day—cleaning the mess that someone else had created.

"It's all karma," she whispered to herself. With that thought, she forced herself to understand that she had to go through all of this in order to reach the end, in order to make it to a better side. She stood up, gripped the mop tightly, and turned back into the bathroom.

"I *can* do this. I *will* do this," she kept whispering to herself as she started to clean. "This is all going to be over one day."

The first bathroom was spotless by the time she finished, and Liling couldn't point out any problems or faults. So, Xiaofan moved onto the next. One after another, Xiaofan eventually managed to clean most of the bathrooms, and Liling approved them when she finished. The entire day had passed, and Xiaofan hadn't eaten *anything* while the rest of the girls finished their lunch hours ago. She was tired, aching, and she desperately wanted sleep, but she still had two more to go. It took her an hour to finish cleaning the last of them, but when Liling found a speck—a tiny little piece of dirt—on the floor, she refused to feed her.

"But—I've worked the entire day!" Xiaofan pleaded. "Please don't do this!"

"Rules are rules. You have to *earn* your food with honesty and hard work," Liling firmly said as she mopped up the speck of dirt that she found. She set the mop head down with a wincing *clang*! "You don't get food when you don't work properly. Now go to your room!"

Tears started to roll down Xiaofan's face as she ran to her room and slammed the door behind her. Everyone heard it, but the girls knew that this was going to happen. This was something that Liling *always* did to the new girls. Luckily, they'd all saved small amounts of food from their own meals and were waiting for her to come upstairs to eat. Liling never checked on them, especially after sunset, so they didn't have to worry about getting caught.

Xiaofan was crying her eyes out on her bed when the girls knocked on her door.

"Not now!" Xiaofan yelled. "Leave me alone!"

The girls looked at each other with concern. They didn't take Xiaofan's behavior to heart as they all understood how taxing all of this was for her. They knocked again, softer this time.

"We have food for you," Fia said in a cheery voice. "You have worked really hard today, so come eat."

"We all saved a little bit of our own food for you," Suki added, hoping that it'll convince Xiaofan to open up.

The moment she heard that, Xiaofan lifted her head. It was in that moment that she came to the realization that she was repeating the same behavior that led her into this mess—the same behavior that made karma come after her. She was projecting her problems and emotions onto others, and she'd promised herself that she'd change. She gathered the little strength she had remaining and opened the door to all the smiling girls.

"I'm sorry," Xiaofan sniffled.

"It's okay; it's been a hard day for you," Fia reassured her. They all gave her a group hug as they entered her room.

"You don't have to apologize," Luna whispered.

Lanying agreed, "We have all been through this. Liling always manages to point out a fault."

Suki added, "Yes, and when she cannot find any, she intends to create them."

Xiang jumped in. "And most of the time, she plots them herself. Nobody gets the opportunity to eat on their first day. We've all experienced it, and that's why we're here for you."

"Thank you. This means a lot to me. I don't even know how I'm going to pay you back for all of this." Xiaofan wiped away her tears with a sleeve.

Fia waved her off. "There are no paybacks in this family."

After that day, their friendship tightened. Even though every day at the orphanage was a pain, the wrath of Liling was never a surprise. It felt like it was her life's mission to make the lives of the girls miserable, but at the end of the day, they all had each other to lean on, to share secrets with, and to vent about their problems with. They'd created their own little family at a place that was known to be a shelter for those without one.

They'd found a family in each other.

Xiaofan slowly began to come out of her shell. She became more expressive and talked about things that bothered her or meant a lot to her. It was hard for her to leave the comfort of the castle and find a new home here, but her life before was a false reality, and what she had found here—in a group of young girls—was something that she could never have experienced in her old life.

TEN YEARS SOON PASSED IN THE BLINK OF AN EYE. THE GIRLS had all grown up, even though much of the orphanage hadn't changed. They were all still subjected to extreme lengths of physical and mental abuse, the living standards remained detrimental, and the structure of the orphanage had corroded. The town was always taken over by extreme winters, and there would be long, endless days without sunlight or blue skies. Most of the days at the orphanage were full of sorrow and remorse, only a small percentage being somewhat close to comfort.

The past decade had made Xiaofan learn a lot about the town, the orphanage, and their headmistress. She understood emotions that she never knew existed, half of them just extensions of melancholy. Pure happiness was something that she had forgotten about, and the only thing she cherished about that phase of her life was the friendship she had with the orphan girls.

They would often gather at night just to talk over saved food and stolen hot chocolate. They once decorated their rooms, but Liling marched upstairs unannounced one evening and ripped down all the artwork that they had made. They never tried to stand up for themselves because Liling held the power over their livelihoods. She could do anything she wanted to harm the girls. She refused to fix the nails coming out of the floorboards, and the girls would often end up getting injured. She also refused to fix the rooftops, causing freezing rain to pour inside.

Liling was coldblooded. It almost seemed like she had no humanity in her, no sense of empathy for the girls.

Xiaofan hadn't been in touch with her powers once since leaving the castle ten years prior. She almost felt like they didn't exist anymore because she had been nothing but numb for the longest time. She only felt sorrow, and in order to take control over her power, she had to experience *different* emotions. Here at the orphanage, nobody knew that Xiaofan had a magical power. She never mentioned or projected them because they were something from her past, and she didn't want to remember them.

On top of it all, even though Xiaofan was fond of the girls at the orphanage, she often felt like she was everyone's second choice. The girls had been together long before her arrival, and even though they welcomed her with open arms, she felt like a gap was present between them. A gap of time and things that she could not comprehend.

Maybe she was overthinking this. Maybe it was her insecurity taking control over her, but she felt like everyone prioritized others over her. She always felt like she was constantly the last one picked, and that always brought back painful memories. She remembered how her father chose her brother over her and sent her away. She often thought about how her mother never reached out, never wanted her back from the fake training school that she was attending. Perhaps she *did* know where Xiaofan really was and just didn't care. Maybe she only wanted betterment for herself, and standing up to Qianfan or coming to get her daughter would have only created problems for her.

"Good for her," Xiaofan would always say whenever she thought about her mother.

The town that she was in was known for its darkness and practices of black magic. They had a tendency to worship the evil spirits and let them roam free in this worldly realm. There were brothels on every street, drunk men lying on every corner. The town was not safe for *anyone*, especially young girls. Even if the girls *did* finish their chores early and were permitted to leave, they always confined themselves within the walls of the orphanage. Angry, evil spirits roamed there, and Liling was the center of it all.

Liling was the most wicked individual that Xiaofan had ever come across, and she *never* let the girls out of her sight. Xiaofan often thought about Liling's life before she became the headmistress of this torture chamber. Maybe, like her, Liling had also endured great extents of pain, and she was putting up a façade to hide all her scars.

Xiaofan, Xiang, Luna, Suki, and Fia were all seventeen now, while Lanying was just a year younger. The orphanage had five beautiful teenage girls residing there, and the place had become a hot topic of discussion in town. Drunk men would show up at the door, banging on it loudly to let them in. Strangers crept around the orphanage's grounds and lurked across the street. Liling would even receive invitations to events that would allow the girls to interact with the men of town.

But the headmistress always declined the invitations, even when she was being offered handsome amounts of money. The girls were still her responsibility, and despite how much she hated them, she still protected them from the darkness looming outside.

The girls woke up one morning to see complete darkness outside. The sky was covered with thick, dark gray clouds that were about to welcome a hail storm at any minute. They all came out of their rooms and assembled for breakfast.

"Something feels different today," Suki muttered while trying to light the oil lamps in the entrance hallway.

"Yeah, you're right," Xiaofan replied. "It feels like something really bad is ahead of us."

"Let's *not* let that thought ponder over us." Suki smiled and went to grab breakfast—boiled beans and black tea.

"Oh, how delightful!" Fia commented sarcastically as she filled her plate.

"At least we aren't being starved to death," Suki commented.

"Suki, take a break from all your positivity and gratitude for once," Fia muttered. "I just want to feel what I feel right now—ungrateful."

"I second that!" Luna chuckled with a mouthful of beans.

Xiaofan felt the air change, and she feared for something unknown. Most of the time, she stayed silent during their conversations. She kept her opinions to herself and only answered if someone asked her a question or spoke to her directly. The girls understood that about her and always respected her space.

After ten minutes, they all went to different corners of the orphanage to complete their chores. They had a rule—start early, finish early. But this rule never meant much because the chores usually took all day to complete, and after that, they had to study, leaving them exhausted.

The sky grew darker as hours passed by, the roaring thunder leaving the weak walls of the orphanage startled. After a while, it started to hail, and the ceiling inside their rooms started to leak.

"Wipe up the floors! There's water everywhere!" Liling demanded.

The girls looked at each other, all with no will to grab the brooms and wipe the floors clean. But they knew they couldn't go against Liling, so each of them grabbed their supplies to mop... except Xiaofan. Her stomach cramped and squeezed. Her arms sagged with fatigue. Her head spun from the dizziness and lack of nutrition. She couldn't do one more second of cleaning. She *wouldn't*.

"No," she whispered, looking down at the floor as her stomach growled.

"What did you say?" Liling took a step toward her, her face tight.

"I said, *no*. No, I am *not* doing this. I'm tired, and I'm hungry. I'm *not* going to spend another hour cleaning these stupid floors on an empty stomach!" she yelled.

"Watch your tone!" Liling spat before her lips curled into a snarl. "You are going to regret this."

"Bullshit! The only thing I regret is staying here under your supervision. You don't have a heart; you don't care. You never have!" Xiaofan screamed.

"Then what are you waiting for? Leave!" Liling suggested with a snicker. "You think *I* don't care? Wait until you go outside these walls. People will eat you alive. They're ready to hunt a pretty princess like you."

Xiaofan laughed in disbelief. "How can a monstrosity like you even *think* about talking about the evils of life? I would rather live on the street than under your command for one more second!" Xiaofan bellowed.

Liling could not accept the disrespect, and she had reached the verge of her patience. How *dare* she question her? How *dare* she call her a *monster*? After all she had done for the little ungrateful twit—how dare she?

Liling grabbed her by the shoulder and pushed her out of the orphanage into the pouring rain. The girls called out behind them, and Xiaofan fought against her grip, but nothing could stop the storm of the headmistress.

"Your wish is my command. Go die on the street for all I care," Liling spat as she kicked Xiaofan outside. She locked the door behind her when she came back in and ordered the girls to go to their rooms.

"Please, let her in! She'll freeze to death!" Fia cried out.

"Anyone who wants to advocate for her can go join her outside," Liling declared, thinking that threat would shut them up. But Fia took a step forward.

"Fine. I will go then. I will *not* leave her alone."

"I will, too!" Luna added, stepping up beside Fia.

"Me, too," Xiang murmured.

"Yes. Us, too," Suki and Lanying agreed.

They all unlocked the door without waiting for a response from Liling, and they marched outside. The door slammed shut behind them, but they didn't bother turning around to look. They searched everywhere for Xiaofan, but she was nowhere to be seen. The pouring rain had turned into a slight drizzle, but it was still very dark.

Liling stared at them from her room's window,

hoping they would come to their senses. She snickered to herself as she watched them wander aimlessly. Her mind already started coming up with a list of things that she could do to punish them after this.

After about an hour, Liling walked over to the entrance and opened the door, indicating that the girls were allowed back in. Xiaofan was nowhere to be found, and the freezing rain was beginning to send shivers throughout their bodies, forcing the girls to give up and retreat back inside.

"Where could she be?" Fia muttered.

"I don't know," Xiang whispered.

"I hope she's safe." Luna looked over her shoulder as they walked in, leaving the door open for Xiaofan to follow if she was still out there.

"Back already?" Liling chuckled. "Where's the rebel? Hiding behind you all?"

All of them just stared at her.

Fia broke the silence. "She's not here."

She's not—? Liling's mind repeated those words again and again. What if someone had taken her? What if she became a victim of something unspeakable? Questions started to cloud her mind, and she left for her room without punishing the girls, without saying a word.

Hours ticked by into the night, every second leading them toward the possibility of never seeing Xiaofan again. Fia paced back and forth in the hallway while all the other girls sat by the fireplace, something they were never allowed to do. The room was filled with silence, and the air was getting harder and harder to breathe as it soaked up their anxious thoughts.

"We should have said something," Fia mumbled and sat down by the fireplace. "We were too late. We should've said something when she stood up to Liling."

Nobody answered at first, exchanging glances with each other instead.

But then Suki spoke, "We *did* go after her; we were just too late."

Fia wiped her tears away. "Yeah, too late."

Lanying and Luna remained silent, sitting close to each other.

"This is on her; it's not our fault. Her ungrateful attitude went to her head. Girls like us don't have a choice but to compromise with reality," Xiang whispered quietly. "We can't blame ourselves."

"Well, we can't blame her, either. She stood up for us!" Fia argued.

"Yelling at each other isn't going to help bring her back! Get over yourself!" Xiang yelled, leaving Fia speechless. After a moment of silence, Xiang sighed, defeated. "I didn't mean that."

Fia mumbled, "I'm sorry."

Now it was Xiang's turn to let the tears fall. "I-I just don't know what's happening," she stuttered.

"It's okay," Fia replied and reached over to give her a hug.

While Fia and the girls were praying for a miracle, Liling was out looking for Xiaofan. She waited hours and hours for her to show up, and when she didn't, she went out to search for her herself. Maybe she really *did* have a heart.

Liling was also an orphan, still bearing the scars of a childhood spent inside an orphanage. She was subjected to harassment and abuse several times during her early teen years. And now, she was stuck running the very same orphanage that had done her dirty. The memories she had in here were not something she wanted to remember, and she only took her rage out on the orphans to protect herself. All these years, she tried to hold it together, tried to keep up that wall of apathy. But the moment that Xiaofan didn't come back in, she couldn't help but fear that she'd face the same tragedies that Liling had as a child.

She roamed the streets and knocked on several doors, asking if anyone had seen a young adolescent girl. After searching for several hours and coming up empty, her mind convinced her to give up and head back to the orphanage. Her steps toward the orphanage were slow, and her mind was filled with guilt. She entered the main gate and closed it gently behind her. Her eyes continued to look around but failed to detect anything that would lead her to Xiaofan.

But just as she reached the front door, she heard a strange sound coming from the back yard. She slowly walked around the building and closed her umbrella, ready to use it as a weapon in case someone or something jumped at her. Suddenly, she saw a piece of white cloth that looked very similar to what Xiaofan was wearing. She ran toward the cloth and found the girl lying on the ground, unconscious and with a high temperature.

"My child! My sweet, sweet child!" Liling whispered, thanking the sky for keeping her protected from the predators outside. She held Xiaofan's lifeless body in her arms and carried her to the front entrance.

Liling pushed open the door and rushed toward the fireplace. The girls quickly jumped up at her sudden appearance before moving aside when they realized who the headmistress was carrying. Liling was completely soaked from the rain, and with apprehension visible on her face, she placed Xiaofan on top of the warm blankets that Fia had laid down on the floor. The girls surrounded her after running to grab more blankets and some hot tea. They covered her and gave her everything that she would possibly need to fight a severe cold.

An hour later, Xiaofan woke up to find everyone settled around her.

"You're okay," Fia muttered with dried tears around her eyes.

"Here, get up. Eat some soup," Xiang ordered her.

"Liling made it for you," Lanying revealed.

Xiaofan felt too weak to get up on her own, so Suki helped her sit up and held her tight so she could focus on the bowl. "Is it poisoned?" she asked.

Everyone stared at each other.

"No," Liling answered politely, stepping back into the room.

Xiaofan gave her a look of uncertainty, but she sipped at the warm soup, nonetheless. It was too fragrant to ignore.

"Oh, it's very... good," Xiaofan whispered, and then a laugh bubbled out of her.

Xiaofan looked at Liling over the top of her bowl, remembering everything that she had heard while she was unconscious. She had heard *everything*—how the headmistress was worried about her and how she went out into the pouring rain to look for her. Maybe Liling was a different version of herself now. Xiaofan finished her soup, and gracefully thanked Liling for taking care of her.

The headmistress escorted all the girls back to their rooms for bed. When she got to Xiaofan's room, she sat down beside her after tucking her in.

"What happened?" she asked quietly.

"What?" Xiaofan looked up from above her thick blankets.

"When you were outside. Did something happen?"

Xiaofan paused. "No," she admitted. "After you left, I went to the back yard and slept."

"Okay, good." Liling sighed with relief, chuckling at the silliness of the whole situation and her long, unnecessary search. The girl had been in the back yard all along.

She went back to her own room after wishing the orphan a good night and turning off the lights.

But Xiaofan lied awake in the dark. She had lied to Liling and the others. Something *did* happen while she was out in the wild. But she wasn't ready to talk about it. Plus, she sensed that Liling change for the better because of this, and she would blame herself if the truth ruined it.

When Liling left her outside, she just stood there, regretting taking a stand for the girls and for herself. She was afraid, but a part of her was determined to prove her point. She saw the door close before her very eyes and heard Liling locking it, and that's when it clicked—there was no going back.

Xiaofan looked around and saw a group of men leering at her while smoking cigars and drinking from glass bottles. She always watched over this street from her room's tiny window, but standing here felt different. She felt eyes all over her, making her feel uncomfortable, something she hadn't felt in a very long time.

She started walking toward the left side of the street. The sky had grown darker, and it almost felt like it was midnight. The eyes followed her with every step she took, and after a while, she noticed that a trio of men were following her. There was no one else on these streets as Xiaofan's steps became quicker, but the faster she tried to walk, the closer the footsteps behind her got.

She started to run, her heart pounding loudly in her ears. *Mother, protect me,* she prayed, when suddenly, she felt someone grabbing her by the waist.

"Looks like the little lamb has lost her way," one of the men whispered into her ear.

"Get your hands off of me!" Xiaofan screamed.

"Run! Run... *if you can*," the man laughed.

The other two men had disappeared, and Xiaofan knew she had to fight for herself; she didn't have much time. She screamed again, but there was no one around to hear her. Rage—that's all she felt, and after struggling to get out of the man's grip, her body started to grow warmer and warmer.

Suddenly, her hands turned into two flaming fireballs that burnt the man's wrists and his upper arms, which were wrapped around her. He screamed in hysteria and loosened his grip on her. She could see the fear in his eyes and felt herself smile.

"Who's the little lamb now?" Xiaofan yelled as she pointed her hands toward him and started to throw balls of fire. Seeing this, the man turned and ran for his life.

Xiaofan calmed down after she saw him disappear into the darkness. Her hands turned back to normal when her heart rate eventually settled. She smirked at her warm hands, feeling the magic within her pulsing and flowing with life.

She rushed back toward the orphanage, not wanting to attract any more attention on the dark street. Xiaofan was shivering, traumatized, even if her magic *did* just save her life. She stood in front of the door, but she didn't have the mental stability to confront Liling, so she went around to the back yard instead.

What just happened? A few minutes ago, she was covered in fireballs, and now she felt like she was going to freeze to death. With her thoughts racing, she started to feel dizzy, and before she knew it, she fell unconscious on top of the wet grass.

When she regained consciousness, she was back inside, surrounded by Liling and the girls of the orphanage. They offered her love and comfort; they prayed for her to get better.

The last few hours had slipped her mind, and she couldn't remember anything after she had fainted except for the cries of Liling. And the sight that she saw when she opened her eyes again was something she had never seen before in her ten years of living here. The incident had brought them all together and changed Liling for the better. There was no way she was going to ruin all that.

But in the quiet solitude of her own room, the trauma came flooding back.

CHAPTER FOUR

The incident had an impact on everyone after that night, especially Liling. She completely changed the menu of the orphanage to meals that the girls liked, took away all their chores, and even hired someone to fix the roof. She started treating them better, splurging on them, and told them that the only thing they had to focus on were their studies.

Liling realized after that fateful night that she was never at peace, that she was only torturing herself by projecting her emotions onto the girls. She knew she had to make their experiences at the orphanage better so they'd never have to go through what she went through. She knew she'd only be at peace after she made things right for these girls.

The girls had also gotten stronger after that night, and they realized how much they loved each other after almost losing Xiaofan.

Xiaofan, on the other hand, did what she did best —put on a show. She claimed she was fine. She laughed and joked around, but deep down, she could still feel the hands wrapped around her, suffocating her. She would lock herself in her room for hours and cry, and she'd constantly have nightmares of men laughing at her replaying over and over inside her head.

Her emotions were all over the place, and she couldn't control them *or* her power. The dark shadows that used to loom over the orphanage were slowly being lifted, but they were all transferred to Xiaofan.

Three months passed by before the girls and Liling finally started noticing her isolation, but no one reached out to her. They just assumed it was something to do with her past, and they chose to leave her alone because that's what Xiaofan usually preferred.

One day, Xiaofan heard a noise coming from outside her room, a noise she'd never heard before. She peeked out the window and saw carriages passing by, all with royal guards sitting inside them. The carriages stopped at a distance, and the guards stepped off. They were dressed in formal black uniforms, and all of them had swords beside them.

The guards cleared the street and took their positions on both sides, capturing Xiaofan's attention.

A few minutes passed, and nothing more happened, but when Xiaofan started to turn away, a much larger carriage—one led by white stallions—showed up and stopped right in front of the orphanage.

The guards tried to clear the surrounding streets, but their presence only brought in a larger crowd. Men, women, and children stood on both sides of the road, eager to know what was happening.

A man then walked out of the large carriage and loudly announced, "Make way for Queen Xiuying!"

"Xiuying?" Xiaofan heard herself say. "Queen? How?"

The sister her parents had abandoned was now a queen? She couldn't understand what was happening as she glimpsed from the tiny window of her room, hearing chants of people praising the queen. Xiaofan decided to ignore all that was happening because she knew that there was no way her sister would come all the way here just to see her. She told herself that this had *nothing* to do with her and forced herself to sleep.

Xiaofan woke up a few hours later to find Xiuying sitting on the side of her bed. She slowly opened her eyes and rubbed at them—she must still be inside her own dream. But Xiuying was really there, grinning down at her and holding her hand. Xiaofan sat up.

"Hi, Sister," Xiuying greeted gently.

"Hi...," Xiaofan replied with great hesitation.

Is she really here for me?

Was this all a lie?

Was she ever abandoned?

Xiuying stood up and took a deep breath, trying to think about how to start the conversation. "Xiaofan, I am your sister."

Xiaofan was now looking down at her hands and noticed that Xiuying had a tiny mark there, too. She stayed silent for a few seconds before whispering, "I know."

"How do you know?" Xiuying asked, raising a brow in question.

The flood of memories rushed back to Xiaofan—everything that had haunted her since she was eight years old. She was a different person now, but with her sister standing right in front of her... she didn't feel so alone anymore.

"A maid from our castle told me about you, and when I questioned our father and tried to ask about you, he sent me here. He resented me for talking back, for disobeying his rules," Xiaofan replied with tears burning her eyes.

Xiuying sat down beside the bed, her eyes glowing with unshed tears of her own. "I'm sorry that you had to suffer because of me."

"No, not because of you," Xiaofan continued. "He finally has a son, what he's wanted all along. With a baby boy in his life, he no longer needed me. I just hope he becomes a true father for our brother."

"People like him can *never* become parents. I met

him two years ago. And let me tell you, *nothing* has changed."

"What do you mean?" Xiaofan perked up.

"Mother and Father reached out to me when I got married to the Prince of Baoshu. The letter that they wrote to me mentioned you. I only went back to our kingdom to meet you, but you weren't there. Father told me how he'd sent you away, and I've been looking for you ever since. From island to island, from shelter to shelter."

Xiuying looked up at her sister, that warm smile blooming once more.

The words that came out of Xiuying's mouth calmed Xiaofan for the first time in months. Someone was there for her, someone who cared, someone who didn't give up on her. That's all she ever wanted, and Xiuying, the sister she'd never known, had given her that.

Xiaofan started to cry when she heard her sister explain her struggles of finding her, and Xiuying comforted her, assuring her that things were only going to get better from here on out. Xiuying sat beside Xiaofan on her bed with a warm blanket wrapped around her. She wiped her tears away as she finished her story, and they started to talk as sisters and friends. They had so much to catch up on.

Xiuying told her about her own life, how her birth was mourned as a death at Jinu, how she was brought up by a nanny named Mei, how she felt neglected and abandoned, how she survived suicide, and how Mei stood up for her.

She explained in detail her journey to the island of Naje. She talked about Huizhong and his letters, along with her new life on the island. She mentioned Hua, and the way she took her in and showered her with love and affection. She told her about her best friend, Meili, and how Zhang magically appeared in her life. Finally, she talked about her life at her new kingdom, her wedding, her visit to their parents, and how she ended up here.

Xiaofan was bewildered. Her older sister went through extreme measures just to reach her, and Xiaofan felt waves of guilt rush through her bones for merely suffering alone at the orphanage this whole time. It had consumed her life, but still, it seemed like nothing compared to Xiuying's life.

"I have dreamt about this day every night for the past two years. I'm grateful that I have finally found you, and from here on out, I will be there for you." Xiuying took her sister's hand and squeezed it gently. Xiaofan looked up from their embrace, only to meet Xiuying's serious gaze. "I won't let you stay here any longer."

This reunion brought a sheer sense of felicity for both of the sisters. Looking at the dreadful conditions of the town and the eclipse that it sheltered within, Xiuying refused to leave her sister in this filth. Even though the town itself was home to obscurity and sin, the orphanage felt like an escape from all evil. Xiuying was amazed to see the bond that all the girls and the headmistress had, and was completely oblivious to what had happened in the past.

After the heartfelt exchange, Xiaofan accepted Xiuying's offer to join her at her new castle and leave this nightmare behind. But the girls. She had made true friends during her stay, and whether she wanted to admit it or not, she was going to miss them. Their secret getaways, shared sorrows, and cheery chatters. They were a part of her life; they were her sisters before Xiuying showed up. They gave her hope and a family when she needed them the most. She would never forget that.

Xiaofan packed her belongings into a small wooden box, suddenly realizing how little she had. The orphanage had taken plenty from her, but it also made her understand herself in a better way. She was able to recognize her *true* self and grow into someone stronger. The town and its people made her take control over her power and helped her become humble. The prideful Xiaofan who walked in a decade ago was no longer there, and maybe *that* was the most valuable thing that she could bring with her.

The door to Xiaofan's room opened with a subtle knock. It was Xiuying.

"Ready to leave?" she whispered with a grin, and Xiaofan nodded.

This was the last time that Xiaofan would be in this tiny, damp room. The room had been home to bitter memories at first, but it also housed many good ones with the girls, and eventually, with Liling, who had turned into a loving caretaker. She stood in the doorway and gave it one last look before pulling the door shut behind her, leaving her past and her dark memories behind.

She walked down the staircase to find everyone standing there to wish her a happy farewell. All her friends were standing in line, holding presents that they wanted her to have. Fia handed over a painting that she had made of all the girls.

"So you don't forget us," Fia mumbled, sniffling.

"I'll *never* forget you guys," Xiaofan whispered.

Xiang gave her a knitted scarf that had all of their initials embroidered onto it.

"This is beautiful." Xiaofan took it gratefully, smiling at her friend.

Lanying, Luna, and Suki brought out a cake that they had baked for Xiaofan, with frosting on it that said, *You will always be family.* Xiaofan found herself speechless; it was the people that she was going to miss the most. Even if she didn't accept this place as her home, she still had a family here.

Liling hugged her. "You have changed things for the better. Thank you."

They all walked Xiaofan out to the main gate of the orphanage, and the girls called for a group hug one more time before Xiaofan stepped onto the carriage with her sister. Xiuying was surprised to witness all the emotions, but she was glad that Xiaofan had the support of these girls when she couldn't be there to support her sister. Her happiness caused her own power to stir inside her, and suddenly, golden shimmering dust appeared in the air, leaving everyone in awe.

Within a matter of seconds, the area surrounding the orphanage was covered with bushy green trees. The grass turned green, and flowers of all kind began wrapping around the walls of the orphanage. As a gesture of good will, Xiuying handed over two boxes filled with gold coins to Liling, and the headmistress promised that she would look after the girls and their well-being.

Xiaofan was stunned, speechless. The power that Xiuying had was simply... beautiful.

I wish I were like her, Xiaofan thought to herself, admiring the flowers around her and admittedly feeling a little envious at the same time.

Xiuying boarded the carriage after Xiaofan, and they were escorted by guards to the harbor. Xiaofan peeked from the door's window and noticed that nothing had changed about the town. It looked just like it did the day she came here—the harbor was in a horrible condition, and there were no boats around except for the three that belonged to Xiuying. History was repeating itself, and Xiaofan found herself going back to royalty, feeling the same emotions that she felt whenever she thought of that word.

The ship began to set sail, and the town started to shrink in the distance, but Xiaofan kept her eyes on it until she could no longer make out the buildings.

"Xiaofan?" Xiuying whispered as she stepped up beside her. "Are you okay?"

Xiaofan nodded but stayed silent, and Xiuying was starting to notice her sister's scars. The orphanage, the kingdom, their father—they had all ruined her. And it was time for Xiuying to heal those wounds and make it all better.

"Let me show you your room!" Xiuying turned, and Xiaofan followed her.

They walked down the deck to an enormous room, one that was way bigger than any of the rooms at the orphanage. It held a single bed with light pink silk sheets and drapes, there were pink roses placed inside a vase on a wooden desk beside some books, and the room was lit with several oil lamps.

"Y-You d-didn't have to do all this," Xiaofan stammered.

"I did, Sister. I did," Xiuying replied, beaming at her. "Now relax! I'll be back for you in a bit." With that, she turned toward her own room and left Xiaofan alone to gather her thoughts.

Xiaofan took a deep breath, closed the door, and sat down on the bed. All of this was so surreal! She stood up and walked over to the table, picked up a book, and flipped it over in her palms. It was thick and heavy, something she hadn't seen in ages. She remembered a time when she used to read books like a maniac, but now she couldn't find it in herself to concentrate. Her passions had been taken away by the wretched town over time.

She placed the book back in its place and walked back to the bed that felt foreign to her. It was so soft, so clean, nothing like her bed at the orphanage. It was... strange, and she felt like an intruder in her own room.

A BIT LATER, XIAOFAN WOKE UP TO A KNOCK ON HER DOOR.

"You may enter," she called out groggily.

Xiuying entered with a shiny silver tray in her hands. She hopped onto the bed with her legs crossed as she faced Xiaofan.

"Did I wake you?" she asked.

"No, I was already up," Xiaofan lied.

"Great! I baked some moon cakes for you," Xiuying revealed giddily as she uncovered the tray.

Xiaofan's eyes widened with delight. "They look delicious, but what are these again?"

"Moon cakes are a specialty in our kingdom, preferred during moments of delight and celebration," Xiuying explained.

Xiaofan beamed and took a bite.

"This is amazing!" Xiaofan moaned against the sweet warmth of the cake coating her tongue. She took another bite. "I could have this every day!"

Xiuying laughed. "Well, I'm sure you're going to admire the kingdom and its people just as well."

Xiaofan looked down all of a sudden. She didn't know what to say nor what to expect. Xiuying paused, noticing her hesitation. She reached out and touched her sister's hand.

"I know this is scary for you. It's a big change, and I went through something similar, so I can understand the emotions that you're going through. I didn't believe Zhang either when he assured me that the kingdom was going to welcome me with open arms, but I saw it for myself. You *will* be welcomed, like you are coming home, Xiaofan. I promise you." She squeezed her hand, and Xiaofan's chewing slowed as she looked at her. "Everyone has been worried for you, ever since we found out about you. Even though they haven't met you, the people of Baoshu have been eagerly awaiting for your arrival. And I'm sure they are going to love you when they meet you in person." Xiuying smiled, but Xiaofan stayed silent for a few seconds.

"I don't know who I am, and I don't like who I was before at the kingdom. I was filled with uncontained pride, and that's what led me to my downfall. Like Father said, it's karma."

"What do you mean?" Xiuying asked.

Xiaofan took a slow, heavy breath. "Father believed that the way he treated you was the reason why his second child was a daughter, too. He deemed that the universe was punishing him for the way he treated you. He acknowledged that what he did was evil, but he felt no regret; in order to reverse the vengeance of karma, he tried his best to treat me right. He gave me everything that I wanted and acted like a loving father should. And then, after years of pretense, he was given a son. His third child was a blessing for him after all this time, and in his eyes, karma was on his side again. After our brother's birth, things changed. His attention shifted, and he abandoned me," Xiaofan paused and gasped for air.

"I wasn't an amiable person at the kingdom," she continued after catching her breath. "I treated people like they were debris. The grandeur, the pretense of love, and all the privilege had gone to my head. I lost count of how many people I've mocked, offended, and insulted. I was *not* respected; I was feared, and I looked at everyone like they were beneath me. Just like Father did. That's why karma did what it did to me—pride dragged me to the pits of despair. I don't want to be like that again, Xiuying."

"Xiaofan, maybe you're seeing all this in the wrong light. You are afraid that royalty is going to make you prideful again, but you are also forgetting that you can be proud *without* being vain. There is nothing wrong with being proud of yourself; it's something that human beings are particularly prone to. You need to understand that you *can* be humble *and* proud of yourself, all at the same time. You are no longer who you were at the kingdom, right?" Xiaofan's eyes flickered. "Time has passed, and you've grown to be a wonderful person. You were a child back then. You have learned so much, stayed humble, and made great friends. You are not who you were. People change, and *you* have changed."

Xiuying squeezed Xiaofan's hands tightly, and for the first time since they met, Xiaofan squeezed back.

Xiaofan finally felt at peace after such a long time. She had kept all this inside for years, and saying it out loud made her feel like a tumor had been removed. She had never seen her situation from the perspective that Xiuying showed her, but with it, the darkness in her heart lightened.

"Thank you," she whispered. "Thank you for everything. And thank you for listening to me."

"What are sisters for?" Xiuying joked, lightening the tension in the room. "You can *always* trust me, Xiaofan. You're the only blood family I have, and I will *always* look out for you. Got it?"

"Got it." Xiaofan grinned and began to munch on the moon cakes again. "These really *are* remarkably delicious."

Xiuying chuckled and poured some tea as they talked about the Baoshu Kingdom, Zhang, and the Wei family.

CHAPTER FIVE

THE JOURNEY TO THE KINGDOM TOOK THREE DAYS, AND THE sisters didn't spend even a minute apart. Xiuying felt like she held the responsibility to make her sister feel at ease, to make her feel at home, just like Zhang did when *she* needed it. Xiuying realized that she was the backbone of the family, and she promised herself that she was *never* going to let her younger sister down, especially after everything that had happened in their lives.

Hours before they were due to reach the kingdom, Xiuying got ready. She wore a pink gown with long bell-shaped sleeves and tiny flowers embroidered onto it, tied her hair into a bun with a tiny tiara, and colored her lips with handmade rosy balm. After she was done, she rushed to Xiaofan's room with a dress that she had selected. It was a purple silk gown with tight sleeves and a collar embroidered with jewels.

"Here! I grabbed this for you when I was leaving the kingdom," Xiuying said with a grin.

Xiaofan blushed as she eyed the dress. "This is beautiful." She held the dress closer to her, but she couldn't ignore Xiuying's smile. "You're being so kind to me," she murmured, heat welling in her chest.

Xiuying laughed and waved her off. "Oh, stop it and get ready. We're about to reach the kingdom!"

Xiaofan's eyes sparkled as she stared at her new dress. She had never worn a gown like this, not even at her own castle. And it felt like such a relief to finally get out of the same rag that she's been wearing at the orphanage. She slid on the dress, let her hair down, applied the balm that Xiuying had given her onto her lips, and she brushed her cheeks with peach powder.

When she was done, she turned around to face the mirror and lightly gasped. She didn't even recognize herself! The last time she looked this pretty was when she was going to attend her brother's welcoming ball. That memory of such a dreadful day would have brought her down normally, but her excitement brushed the thought away. She would've never imagined her life turning out the way it did, and she owed it all to her big sister.

A loud bang sounded outside the ship, and Xiaofan turned away from her reflection.

"We're here," she whispered to herself with a mixture of trepidation and delight.

Her sudden urge to get a glimpse of the kingdom brought her toward the window of her room. One look outside, and she gasped. It was huge! She could see the castle from afar, and the landscape looked like someone had painted it in vibrant flowery shades. This kingdom looked like it came out of a fairytale and was the complete opposite of the town where she had spent a lifetime in.

She swung open her door and slowly went up the stairs to the deck, where she found Xiuying standing at the front of the ship, waving to the people who had gathered while the soldiers and maids transported items from the ship to the carriages. Xiaofan was about to walk up to her, but then something stopped her.

I'm nothing but a mere peasant compared to the great queen.

Xiuying turned her body slightly, and she saw her baby sister with the corner of her eye. She waved her hands abruptly, indicating for Xiaofan to join her.

Xiaofan stepped back, slowly moving her head from left to right. She knew she didn't belong up there in front of the public.

"Nonsense!" Xiuying whispered to herself and rushed to grab Xiaofan. "Come on! What's with all this formality?" She pulled Xiaofan by the wrist and brought her to the front of the deck. The moment she arrived, someone standing on the edge of the harbor loudly announced, “Let’s all welcome Princess Xiao-fan, sister of Queen Xiuying!”

With that, everyone cheered for her, and Xiaofan was taken aback. She never would’ve expected such an overwhelming response from people she didn’t even know. Her heart was filled with happiness, and she started to cry as she squeezed Xiuying’s hand. Her sister smiled at her.

“I told you,” Xiuying lightly teased.

Xiaofan nodded while she waved at the people who were cheering for her, never wanting to forget this sight—the people throwing flower petals at them in celebration, the fragrant aroma lingering in the air, and being able to finally stand next to someone who loved her.

A guard informed them that their carriages were ready, and they stepped off the ship together. The harbor here was different from the one near the orphanage; it was well-constructed, massive, and strong. There were several ships docked on the harbor with huge flags waving the kingdom’s crest.

Xiaofan got into the carriage, and her journey toward the castle began. Passed the harbor, she noticed the busy streets, the tiny homes decorated with dragons, red lamps hanging over every corner, and flowers of every kind that painted the town in rainbow colors. They even passed the market, and she saw how alive the place was with shoppers buying products left and right and kids running around freely. For the first time in years, she felt safe, comfortable, and at peace.

This felt like *home.*

Xiuying stayed silent to let her sister enjoy her moment. The carriages reached the castle soon enough and stopped right outside the grand staircase. Xiaofan and Xiuying climbed out and found armed guards standing on both sides of the staircase, which had a red carpet neatly laid out in the middle of it.

Xiaofan couldn't stop admiring the place as she took a few steps forward. Her eyes were on the castle and its details. The wooden dragon carvings on the doors were something that she had never seen before. Baoshu Kingdom was grand and luxurious, even compared to Jinu, and she found herself overwhelmed by everything in front of her.

They reached the main entrance and were welcomed by Zhang's sisters and their mother. They all hugged Xiaofan and introduced themselves eagerly.

"We're so glad to finally meet you, my dear," Huiqing, Zhang's mother, greeted as she held onto Xiaofan's hands.

"Yes, this is a sight for sore eyes. Xiuying has looked *everywhere* for you," Kyrie declared.

"This calls for a celebration!" Kamari cried.

"Indeed, but where are Zhang and Father?" Xiuying asked, looking around.

"They went on a voyage three days ago to increase

the security of the kingdom. They should be home tonight," Huiqing informed them.

"Zhang *did* mention it before, but I was unaware that they had to leave so soon," Xiuying whispered.

"He didn't know. It was *very* last minute. Don't worry!" Kyrie assured her.

"Yeah! Now let's get ready for that celebratory dinner! Come on, Xiuying, we have lots to do," Kamari added, tugging on Xiuying's hand.

"Alright." Xiuying chuckled.

"In the meantime, I'll show Xiaofan her room!" Kyrie declared and turned to Xiaofan with a beaming smile.

Xiuying, Kamari, and Huiqing went into the kitchen while Kyrie escorted Xiaofan to her room. The girls were both the same age, and a genuine friendship was bound to be born.

"Everything has been so out of place lately with all the wedding preparations and Xiuying being gone. I'm so happy that we found you before my wedding," Kyrie cheerily told Xiaofan.

"Congratulations! When is the wedding? Who's the groom?" Xiaofan asked with surprise and excitement.

"The wedding is in two weeks, and the groom is the Prince of Umai. He's so handsome, and I still can't believe I'm actually getting married to him!" Kyrie squealed and opened the door to Xiaofan's room. "Here we are! And I'm *right* next door if you need anything. I'll let you get settled in before I tell you the rest of my love story." Kyrie winked.

"I can't wait." Xiaofan smirked before Kyrie closed the door behind her.

Xiaofan turned around to see an enormous room that was even more luxurious than the one on the ship had been. The room came with a walk-in wardrobe that was filled with gowns of every color, a tremendous bathroom that had handmade soaps and scented candles scattered about, and a wooden desk by the window with all the essentials.

"Am I in Heaven?" she asked herself and sighed with joy.

She spent the entire afternoon trying on the dresses that were hung inside her closet, and she treated herself with a long, long bath. It was clear that she hadn't forgotten how to treat herself like royalty.

Darkness swept over the kingdom soon enough, and Xiaofan got herself ready for dinner. She hadn't seen Xiuying ever since they entered the kingdom, but Xiuying was the queen of Baoshu, so Xiaofan understood that she had things to take care of. She threw on a lilac gown and tied a matching ribbon around her hair. She then used a little blush to polish her cheeks pink when a knock sounded on her door.

"Come in!" Xiaofan called.

Xiuying popped her head in and entered the room. "You look so beautiful, Xiaofan."

"Thank you, as do you, Sister."

"Do you like your room? Clearly, you have seen the

clothes that I have picked out for you. Do you like them?" Xiuying asked.

"I love them! You have *exceptional* taste." Xiaofan twirled around in her dress to prove her point.

Xiuying chuckled. "I'm so glad that you like them. And you know, if there's anything else you need, just say it."

Xiaofan beamed. "I already have everything I need, thanks to my big sister!"

Xiuying laughed. "Okay, then. Ready to go?"

Xiaofan nodded, and the two of them left for the dining room.

The dining room at Baoshu showcased a beautiful wall with a cherry blossom tree painted on it. Candles were lit up in every corner that made the room shine, and the small flames looked like stars dancing around the large tree. Kyrie and Kamari were already sitting down when Xiaofan and Xiuying joined them.

"So? How does the place look to you?" Kamari asked Xiaofan.

"Amazing! I have never seen such elegance in a room before. Everything looks beyond perfect."

"Can we talk about the wedding now? It's just two weeks away!" Kyrie pleaded.

Xiuying snickered and whispered, "Someone's being impatient."

Kyrie huffed, and soon, they heard footsteps approaching them from behind. Xiuying spun around and saw her husband standing behind her.

"You're back!" Xiuying screamed with excitement and jumped up to hug him.

"I've missed you," Zhang whispered and kissed her on the cheek. He held her for a few minutes before pulling back, just enough to look into her eyes. "You're even more beautiful than when I left."

Kamari coughed to make everyone else's presence known, and then started to laugh hysterically.

"Oh, grow up, will you?" Zhang teased, still holding onto Xiuying.

"I found her," Xiuying whispered, and then Zhang looked around to find Xiaofan standing beside his sisters.

"You're finally here!" He stepped toward her, arms outstretched. "Your sister and I have looked *everywhere* for you. Welcome home!" He gave her a light hug, and while Xiaofan hesitated for a moment, she hugged him right back. "Oh, I almost forgot! I want to introduce you all to someone."

Kyrie glanced around, but no one else was there. "Are you talking about your shadow, Zhang? Or perhaps a ghost?"

The sarcastic tone in Kyrie's voice made everyone laugh, but just seconds later, a tall and handsome brown-eyed man walked into the room.

"Ah, here he is!" Zhang announced. "This is Prince Han Qin of the Shénhuà Kingdom."

Han looked around and smiled at everyone, his eyes on Xiaofan the longest. He was Zhang's oldest childhood friend, so Kyrie and Kamari recognized his face. When he was properly introduced to Xiuying and Xiaofan, Ming and Huiqing entered the room for dinner. The rest of the night was spent talking about Xiaofan's dream of becoming a writer, Kyrie's upcoming wedding, and Zhang's stories from his voyage. For the first time in her life, Xiaofan felt like part of a loving family.

"Women are the leaders of our future. You should join Kyrie when she visits the university," Ming suggested.

Xiaofan's intellectual side was praised by everyone at the table and secretly admired by Han. She didn't exchange any words with Han, but they learned a little about each other as others spoke. Xiaofan found out that Han was the only child born in his kingdom, was passionate about improving living conditions for the unfortunate, and he had come to Baoshu specifically to attend Kyrie's wedding.

THE NEXT MORNING, XIAOFAN FOUND HERSELF THINKING about Han as the sun shone through her window. They had just met, but for some reason, she found herself drawn to him, her heart wanting to pounce out of her chest and run over to him. She was so used to keeping to herself, but there was just something about him that made her want to go against her habit.

"Come in!" she called out when she heard a knock on her door, and Kyrie came skipping into the room.

"Good morning, Sleepyhead!" Kyrie exclaimed in a cheerful tone.

"Morning to you, too."

"Why are you still in bed? We have to visit the university today. Father instructed me to take you there as soon as we're up," Kyrie said.

"Oh, right. I almost forgot." Xiaofan quickly stumbled out of bed.

"Really? I wonder what you could possibly be distracted by." Kyrie winked.

Xiaofan felt her cheeks turn hot. "What do you mean?"

"Oh, please, I saw the way you were looking at Han!" Kyrie teased.

"I wasn't looking at him."

"Yeah, okay." Kyrie snorted. "You're totally in love!"

"I *just* met him, Kyrie. I *can't* be in love. But that reminds me, you still have to tell me *your* love story."

Xiaofan turned toward her wardrobe, hoping that Kyrie would get the hint and change the topic.

"Nice try, but get dressed. I'll tell you on the way."

Kyrie walked out and left Xiaofan alone to choose an outfit that would be suitable for her important day. She'd spent most of her life in a filthy orphanage that she'd almost forgotten how to dress.

"Ready for your big day?" Xiuying asked as she peeked inside the room.

"I think so," Xiaofan replied with a nervous smile.

"Best of luck, Xiaofan. I'm proud to be your big sister."

"Xiaofan, it's time to leave!" Kyrie came running into the room again.

Within minutes, they were inside the royal carriage, and Kyrie revealed that she met her fiancé, Zhao, at Xiuying and Zhang's wedding. It was love at first sight, and he asked for her hand in marriage a month later.

"I never thought I would end up with someone who makes me believe in fairytales. I knew what love was, but I never felt it before I met Zhao. I can talk to him about anything without feeling like he'd judge me. He supports me all the way, and I feel truly blessed."

"You certainly *sound* like you're in love. I'm happy for you," Xiaofan replied, wondering if she would ever experience what Kyrie was feeling. It felt so... genuine.

Xiaofan never expected herself to be with a man, especially not after her traumatic experience with men back at that ruthless town. It scarred her, and she had given up on the idea of love. But after last night, after Han, she wasn't so sure anymore.

When they arrived at the university, Xiaofan found it even more extravagant than the castle. Almost everything was intricately carved in wood, and pillars of spiritual animals lined every building. There were beautiful fountains everywhere she turned, and the blooming gardens were much, much bigger than her orphanage.

"You *must* see the library. It's the largest in the entire world." Kyrie pulled Xiaofan and started running toward the west wing.

"There's so much to see and so little time!"

"After a week, you'll be spending every day in here."

When they walked in, Xiaofan could see books lining every corner of the room, stacked from the bottom all the way to the top. She took a deep breath as she stood there and breathed it all in. The smell of fresh pages, ink, and old books always made her feel at home, and it'd been almost a decade since she stepped foot inside one.

"This is divine," she whispered. Xiaofan wandered around and gathered some books to take home while Kyrie sat down at a wooden desk.

"Han?" Kyrie asked loudly.

He lifted his head, which was buried inside the book that he was reading.

"Kyrie?" Han whispered.

Kyrie walked over to him and sat down beside him. "You *have* always been a nerd, haven't you?" she teased.

"I have. I'm surprised to see you here, though."

"You know me well. I've never been a fan of reading. But I wanted to bring Xiaofan here. She just enrolled."

"Good for her," Han replied, his eyes scanning the room in search of Xiaofan.

"She's right behind you."

“I’m not looking for her.”

“I never said you were.” Kyrie laughed, inviting Xiaofan over to the table. “Xiaofan, look who I found buried under a pile of books!” Kyrie yelled, directing everyone’s attention toward them.

Xiaofan’s heart started to pound against her chest as she heard Kyrie. A part of her hoped that it was Han, but another part of her was nervous to see him again. She gathered her books into her arms and walked toward the table.

Han turned as she approached and couldn’t stop staring at her.

“Hey,” he whispered with a smile.

“Hi,” Xiaofan replied, placing her books onto the table.

“I have no idea why people read. It’s so boring!” Kyrie remarked.

“Only people with a *stable* brain can read. I understand why this doesn’t sit well for you,” Han mocked, causing Xiaofan to chuckle.

“Oh, please!” Kyrie said with a sneer. “I just prefer not to. Why are you here, anyway?”

“I had some spare time on my hands. Don’t worry, everything will still be perfect for your wedding.”

Kyrie rolled her eyes. “Yeah, sure. Anyway, I have to run. Do you mind escorting Xiaofan back to the castle?”

Xiaofan shot daggers at her friend, but before she could interject, Han replied, “It would be my pleasure.”

Silence had taken over after Kyrie threw a wink over at Xiaofan and disappeared. Han offered Xiaofan the seat in front of him, and they both started to read without saying a single word to each other. Xiaofan went through all her books, one after another, reading the pages with transcendent enthusiasm while Han was only pretending to read. He glanced up at her every now and then, and admired how passionate she was.

"Han?" Xiaofan murmured, waiting for him to respond. But her voice had gone unheard as his mind was busy thinking about her over a blank page in his book.

"Han?" she said a bit louder, and his head popped up.

"S-Sorry, did you say something?"

"Do you mind if we leave now? I have to reach the castle before sunset."

"Anything for the princess." He smiled at her as he got up from his chair and placed his book back onto the shelf. "Are you taking these books with you?"

"No, I'm done," Xiaofan replied and put hers back as well.

They silently walked out of the library and continued down the hallway.

"So?" Han asked.

"So?" Xiaofan repeated, failing to understand the question.

"You're quite the reader," Han commented. "I must say, I am impressed."

"I can say the same about you."

"I was hardly reading." Han admitted. "I was too busy paying attention to you."

"Why's that?"

"Because I find you fascinating, and I can't wait to learn more about you."

As he looked into her eyes and smiled, Xiaofan could feel herself blushing and quickly turned her head away.

I can't be in love. I can't!

CHAPTER SIX

"You don't talk much, do you?" Han asked on their way back to the castle.

"What?" Xiaofan asked back.

"Well, we've been sitting in this carriage for the past thirty minutes, and you haven't said a single word."

"I do t-talk," she stuttered. "I just don't have anything to say right now."

"Let me help you out, then. I can't let this silence steal away my opportunity to get to know you better."

He grinned at her. "But I feel like we already have so much in common."

"Indeed, we do."

With each sentence, Xiaofan found herself slowly opening up to Han, and she even found herself falling for him more and more after learning about his love for politics and discovering the true meaning of life.

Maybe I shouldn't be so afraid of love after all.

They reached the castle just as the sun was beginning to set. The sky glowed all sorts of pretty colors—pink, orange, yellow, purple. Han stepped out first and opened the door for Xiaofan as the carriage came to a stop.

"I told you we'd be back in time." He smiled.

"You're a man of your word." Xiaofan smiled back.

"I hope I can see you again soon, Xiaofan."

"Maybe," Xiaofan whispered and started to walk toward the grand entrance.

Han found himself grinning from ear to ear as he stood there, watching Xiaofan disappear up the stairs and into the castle. His heart was pulling him in different directions. He wanted to be with Xiaofan as he couldn't stop thinking about her, but his parents—they wanted a different path for him. They wanted a different *girl* for him, a girl they had already chosen, and Han *had* agreed to this... *before* he met Xiaofan. He didn't want to disobey his parents—he couldn't—but after meeting *her*, he was torn.

He was drawn to Xiaofan; he was falling in love with her. Xiaofan felt like home to him from the moment his eyes met hers. However, he realized that he was losing grasp of the reality his parents had designed for him, and the only possible consequence for his affection toward Xiaofan would be unrecoverable heartbreak for them both.

The colors of the sky faded slowly, turning into a shade of darkness that reminded Han of himself. His heart was gambling with fate, and there was *nothing* he could do to stop it. He couldn't get Xiaofan out of his thoughts, his future and his parents' plan tossed to the wayside. The only thing that mattered to him now was seeing Xiaofan again.

Xiaofan's walk to her room was overwhelming. Her thoughts, emotions, and feelings refused to give her peace, and with every step, questions arose in her mind. Was she in love? Were her feelings for him even reciprocated?

She couldn't get his smiling face out of her mind. His voice was on a loop, saying her name again and again. It felt like home when he said it, along with the sparkle in his eyes. And whenever she closed her eyes, she saw his reflection. She opened the door to her room and entered to find Kyrie waiting for her on her bed. She met her eyes with that knowing smirk of hers as Xiaofan closed the door behind her.

"Where have *you* been?" Kyrie teased.

Xiaofan shook her head and chuckled, refusing to fall prey to Kyrie's antics. But Kyrie wouldn't let her get away *that* easily.

"I see that smile... and the light in your pretty, pretty eyes, Xiaofan." She poked and prodded, scooting closer to the edge of the bed. "Spill the beans already!"

Xiaofan sighed dramatically and sat beside her friend. "Alright, alright." After another steadying breath, she told her everything. "The ride back home was long, but it felt like it only lasted minutes. Han started the conversation by saying he wanted to know me, and I hesitated at first. But then—I don't know what happened, but everything shifted. I felt like I had known him my entire life. We talked about everything, and he made me laugh a lot. I don't remember the last time I was this happy. I just... didn't want the journey to end."

"You *do* love him!" Kyrie squealed. "I knew it! I knew it the first time I saw you two staring at each other." Kyrie jumped in excitement. "I'm so happy for you, Xiaofan. And you know, Han doesn't interact with people much, so the fact that he wanted to get to know you shows that he feels something toward you, too."

"Let's not get ahead of ourselves." Xiaofan held up her hands to slow down her friend. "Things usually come crumbling down whenever I hope for them to work out."

That sent a pang through Xiaofan's chest, but she ignored it. It wasn't untrue, but saying it out loud felt... vulnerable in a way.

"It's going to be *different* this time," Kyrie assured

her, but then her eyes flickered to the clock on the wall. "Let's finish this later. We have to go!"

Xiaofan raised a brow at her. "Go where?"

"Tea! Kamari and Xiuying are waiting for us," Kyrie told her, and Xiaofan jumped up. She was eager to see the others, but especially Xiuying.

Evening tea was being served at the grand terrace, with a breathtaking view of the ocean, mountains, and the city.

"This is heavenly," Xiaofan whispered as her eyes glazed over the picturesque surroundings.

Xiuying brewed the tea herself and baked Xiaofan's favorite moon cakes, and Xiaofan couldn't get enough.

"I repeat, I could have these *every day* without getting sick of them." Xiaofan moaned with a stuffed mouth.

"Most of the preparations for the wedding are done," Kamari said.

"All that's left are the food and our dresses," Xiuying added.

"That's great! We had a rather... interesting day, too." Kyrie winked and wagged her brows at Xiaofan.

"Really?" Kamari asked.

"Tell us about it," Xiuying said, setting her teacup down.

Kyrie gave Xiaofan a look as if asking for her permission. Xiaofan rolled her eyes but nodded reluctantly. Kyrie quickly and eagerly told them everything—how they ran into Han, how she came up with the idea to leave them alone, and their conversation during the ride home. She took *all* the credit.

"They wouldn't have even said a word to each other if it wasn't for me." Kyrie pointed at her chest with a wide grin.

Xiaofan rolled her eyes again, but the other two laughed.

"Xiaofan, Han is an exceptional human being. You will be lucky to have him by your side," Kamari said, taking a sip of her tea.

"I also noticed him staring at Xiaofan during dinner, but I thought I was just seeing things," Xiuying admitted. "I still need time to process this because you *are* my baby sister, but I am so glad that this happened." Xiuying smiled over the lip of her teacup as she took another slow sip.

"I don't know... Maybe we're just friends." Xiaofan whispered with flushed cheeks.

"Let's hope not!" Xiuying exclaimed.

"We second that!" Kamari and Kyrie agreed while raising their cups.

"Either way, can we *please* keep this between us?" Xiaofan asked.

Xiuying blinked. "Of course, Xiaofan. My lips are sealed."

"What were we even talking about?" Kamari giggled.

"I'll never say a word," Kyrie said, and everyone laughed.

"Especially you, Kyrie." Xiaofan swatted at her friend.

Xiuying felt euphoric seeing how her sister had found a friend in Kyrie, just like she'd found a friend in Kamari when she first arrived. And she secretly hoped that Han would be the one for her sister.

The rest of the evening was spent discussing color combinations for the wedding dresses. But Xiaofan's heart was elsewhere. She felt like she'd left herself with Han inside the carriage and was longing to see him again.

Xiaofan walked back to her room after the evening team. She'd expected Han to show up, but when he didn't, she felt her heart beginning to ache. Her eyes were locked on the door the whole evening, anticipating his presence and hoping that he would walk in at any minute. She was impatiently waiting to see him again, and she continued to wait for him even after everyone else had left. But her hopes were left empty.

She reached her room with a sense of anguish. The room was darker than usual; only a few of the candles were lit, so she decided to light some more. The darkness always stifled her. She lit one candle at a time, and once she was satisfied, she sat at her desk and propped open a book from the collection in her room.

The Scripted Affection, the cover read. She opened the book and started to read the first page. "To feel estranged has been a constant state of mind for me. To belong somewhere or to a person is all that my heart has ever wanted. I'm always trying to get back to somewhere imaginary. My life feels like an eternity of long-lost longing." She closed the book. The fact that she could understand and relate to every word made her feel trivial, and she didn't want to read anymore.

She wrapped herself in a thick wool blanket and closed her eyes.

The Scripted Affection... was it a sign? Maybe the universe was telling her that she was scripting a tale of love that had absolutely no significance. Maybe she had misread Han's signs, and he really *did* just want to be friends. Her clouded mind whirled, spiraling deeper and deeper toward the darkness. Before she knew it, her body fell victim to that darkness, and her mind quieted.

Xiaofan woke up in the middle of the night covered in sweat and tears. The room had fallen silent around her, and all the candles were blown out by the force of brisk winds that came through the window. The only source of light was coming from the faint shimmer of the moon. Her hands were sweaty and aching; she kept rubbing them together, but the sensations didn't cease. Unable to breathe properly, she got out of bed and ignored the dizziness inside her head as she walked toward the window.

She just had a nightmare that made her re-experience the ill-fated event that transpired outside her old orphanage. Even after all this time, it felt so real, like she was there all over again. She could feel the hands grabbing her, she could hear the sinister laughter, and she remembered how feeble and alone she'd felt. It was something she *never* wanted to experience again, but here she was, struggling to forget. This was the one thing she kept to herself; not even her own sister knew. Perhaps that was the reason why it was weighing her down with iron fists that wouldn't give.

Xiaofan stood by the window but still struggled to breathe properly as thick tears started rolling down her cheeks. She didn't know what to do, how to escape her past and its dark memories, so she went outside. Maybe a walk around the garden would clear her mind.

She silently walked down the hall and out through a side door with a candle in her hand. She stopped when she reached a window that faced the town and showed her a view of the magnificent trees beyond. The atmosphere was still dark, covered by a little fog, but the lights lit inside the homes looked like tiny stars to her. Xiaofan felt too weak to walk any further, so she placed the candle on a step beside her, and she sat down with her head placed on her knees and her arms wrapped around her legs.

She sat there for a few minutes in solitude until she heard footsteps approaching. Her heart started to beat faster, and once again, she struggled to breathe. She was safe inside a guarded castle, but her experience had made her cautious of everything and everyone. She squeezed her eyes shut as the footsteps stopped.

"Xiaofan?"

Her eyes flared open as she heard a voice and

recognized the softness in the tone. It was Han. The last thing she wanted was to let him see her in such a vulnerable state, so she lifted her hand and waved weakly. But Han's worried gaze didn't waver.

"What are you doing here? It's past midnight." He was standing behind her and was able to recognize her even in the dark because of the ribbon that she always wore around her hair.

"I j-just...," Xiaofan stuttered in a weak voice. "I just needed some air."

"Is it okay if I join you?"

Xiaofan wavered, but her voice came out in a quiet whisper. "Yes."

Han sat next to her on the staircase, not giving her a chance to hesitate again.

Xiaofan looked up toward the town, and Han noticed that her eyes were red but shining with the reflection of the town's lights. Her nose had turned pink, and the golden light of the candle was making her look even more pale than she already was. He knew something had happened, something so dreadful that it took the hopefulness away from her voice. All he wanted was to help her, to steal all the tears away and reinstate her laughter. Even if he *had* decided that she would no longer be the source of *his* despair.

After making peace with the decision to stay away from Xiaofan and follow the path that his parents had paved for him, Han couldn't fall asleep. How could he possibly forget the one girl who made him feel alive?

But no matter how much he tried to forget about her and never see her again, he couldn't. It just wasn't in their cards.

The silence between them was comfortable. Han was there for her without needing to say a word. He sat beside her and gazed at the lights sprinkled across town. He wanted to give her some space and respect her privacy, so he decided not to ask any questions. But Xiaofan surprised him with answers, nonetheless.

"I had a nightmare about something that happened to me," she mumbled against her knees. He looked at her for a moment before glancing back toward the lights, giving her time and space to elaborate. "I thought I had moved on from this, and that I would never have to mention it to anyone," she continued, looking down at her hands. "I thought that if I pretended that it never happened, I would start believing that it didn't."

Tears started to roll from her eyes, and Han wanted nothing more than to pull her into a tight embrace and kiss her.

"When I lived at the orphanage, some of the men in town tried to force themselves on me," she admitted, her voice getting thicker and tighter with tears. "I escaped, but the memories are still alive. I can still hear their barks of laughter and feel their hands on me like it happened just yesterday. I hate it. I hate it *so much*, and all I want to do is forget about it. I've tried to move on—to forget—but I can't. I can't—" Xiaofan broke into shivering sobs.

Han was aware of her history; Zhang had told him all about her struggles—her time at the orphanage and how Xiuying found her, but he had never mentioned the men. Han was at a loss for words. He felt rage boiling under his skin, prickling his blood. Life had taken so much from Xiaofan, and he struggled to find words that would make her feel better.

Xiaofan sniffled in the silence. "I've never told anyone, not even Xiuying. I have always been petrified of people questioning my dignity and asking me to relive it by explaining what had happened. It was easier to pretend that it didn't happen at all. But you can only pretend for so long." She wiped at her eyes and cheeks with her sleeve.

"Your secret is safe with me, Xiaofan. And... well, you shouldn't question yourself."

"What do you mean?"

"I mean... this experience of yours and your vulnerability... it has only made me respect you more," Han told her, his voice steadying and growing stronger.

She looked at him as her tears dried. His words brought her comfort, and the darkness swirling in her mind had lifted. The burden of her past had been removed with only a few comforting words from this man she so admired.

"Thank you," Xiaofan whispered.

"For what?" Han peeked at her.

For everything, she wanted to say. "For staying here with me, for listening to me."

Han smiled and shook his head. "You don't have to

thank me for that. I'll always be there for you. You have my word."

Her smile was back, and he thanked the universe at the sight of it. He never imagined that he would feel gratitude over a simple smile, but here he was. And he wished for nothing more. After another moment of silence between them, Xiaofan cleared her throat.

"And what brings you here? Why aren't you asleep?" she asked.

Han shrugged. "I just couldn't, and sometimes I like to walk around to declutter my thoughts."

"Anything you want to share? I can try to alleviate some of it." Xiaofan nudged his arm gently.

"Nah, it's nothing serious." Han shook it off with a wave.

As much as he wanted to, he just wasn't ready to admit his feelings for her and why he couldn't be with her. Especially not when *he* was still confused himself. The chemistry between them was unreal, and he wished he only knew how *she* felt about *him*.

And how could he choose between someone he'd only just met and his own family? He needed help; he needed Zhang. Xiuying was Zhang's future, and Han felt almost certain that Xiaofan was his.

CHAPTER SEVEN

XIAOFAN FELT DIFFERENT WHEN SHE WOKE UP THE NEXT morning. After last night's terror and the paradisiacal interaction with Han, she'd convinced herself that he loved her, too—that she was *finally* going to get her own happy ending. She never thought sharing this unfortunate event would bring the person she loved closer to her. And Han's support, his soft, considerate voice, and his affectionate words were still on repeat in her mind.

But she had to focus today. She had to accompany Xiuying, Kamari, and Kyrie to the dress fitting. She jumped out of bed, got dressed, and hurried to join them for breakfast. Although she was over the moon from last night, she decided to keep the interaction to herself. It wasn't that she didn't trust her sister or her friends; she trusted them with all her heart. But she wanted to keep this moment of sheer happiness a secret, and she wasn't ready to reveal to them the events that led up to that moment.

While the hustle and bustle of the wedding preparations were keeping Xiaofan occupied, Han was trying to get himself out of a dilemma that was making him lose sleep every night.

He was with Zhang at the kingdom's library, impatiently waiting for the right opportunity to bring it up. Luckily, he didn't have to wait long.

"So, what's going on with you and Xiaofan?"

Han paused, and then sat next to Zhang as they stared at the painting of a mystical black dragon on the wall opposite them.

"What do you mean?" Han replied, feigning ignorance.

"Xiuying might have mentioned something."

"Like what?" Han asked, hoping that Xiuying had told him Xiaofan's true feelings for Han.

"Xiaofan is quite fond of you, I assume. I won't go into greater detail because I promised my wife that I wouldn't, but this is a hint for you in case you haven't caught on." Zhang leaned in and lowered his voice. "She is an extraordinary girl."

Han huffed out a dry laugh. "Oh, I know."

"Is there something you're not telling me?" his friend prodded.

Han took a deep breath and admitted *everything* that he had been holding in.

"I *love* Xiaofan. I feel very strongly toward her. I admire her strength, her wisdom, her passions, and her beauty, of course. Every time I interact with her, I cherish every second, and when she's gone, I long for her presence. I have never felt what I feel toward Xiaofan for anyone else. Is that crazy?"

Zhang chuckled, his smile all too knowing. "Well, that's great, right? You love her, and she has feelings for you, too. People who feel affection toward one another belong together. It's that simple."

But Han sighed in distress and curled in on himself. He ran his fingers through his hair as he rested his head on his knees. "It's *not* that simple," he whispered.

"Why not?" Zhang asked.

"You've known me since childhood, and you have met my parents. You know how traditional and strict they are."

Zhang shook his head, that smile still lingering. "Yes, but—"

"But—nothing, Zhang. Being their only child, they have outlined my life for me, made decisions on my behalf, and I have *always* agreed with them. Last year, my father decided that he would soon step down from the throne, leaving it to me. With that, my parents have already decided that the future queen would be the princess of our neighboring kingdom. They asked for her hand in marriage on my behalf *without* even talking to me first. But I am bound to follow the choices that they have made, even if I don't like them."

Zhang's eyes widened at Han's confession, but it didn't end there.

"I trusted their judgment, and at the time, I wasn't even interested in anyone else. But now... since Xiao-fan..." Han tensed, and Zhang's chest constricted for his friend. "I haven't even *met* the other girl, and I don't wish to, now that I have met Xiaofan. But it isn't my choice, and I am to be married in the next six months. I don't know what to do, Zhang. My heart belongs to Xiaofan." He paused, his eyes flickering up at the painting again. "My father wants me to marry a princess so that our kingdom grows stronger. He has given his word, and he's *not* going to take it back, no matter what happens. I cannot forget Xiaofan, and I certainly cannot choose between her and my parents."

Zhang was quiet as he contemplated Han's words. His friend had a reason to be stressed; he couldn't even imagine how he must be feeling. Han was right. His parents were *never* going to understand or backtrack from their words as they never had before. But he couldn't just let go of his own love and affection for Xiaofan... now that he had found it.

"I never thought I'd find love, and now that I have, I don't want to lose it. But... I don't want to lose my family, either," Han whispered, keeping his eyes forward.

"You can't give up, Han. You have to reason with your parents if you truly love her. You have to fight for her." Zhang gently patted his friend's back. "Your parents will be here for the wedding; talk to them. They might understand."

Han remained quiet as Zhang's words tumbled through his mind. It all made sense, and what he said seemed reasonable. He had to do it. He had to tell his parents about Xiaofan, and he could only hope that his parents would listen.

"I'll talk to them when they arrive." Han's muscles visually relaxed.

Zhang smirked and added, "Besides, Xiaofan *is* a princess of *this* kingdom *and* the one where she was born. If your parents want you to marry a princess, then Xiaofan is kind of perfect. And you know, my kingdom is your ally, always."

Han sighed in relief. "I appreciate that."

Zhang stood up and patted Han's shoulder once more. "I will always be here to offer support, you know that. I can't let my best friend go into battle unprepared while fighting for the most important person in his life."

Han chuckled, the entire room lightening with his laugh. "Thanks, truly."

"Don't mention it."

Zhang then excused himself to aid Kyrie's never-ending wedding needs, leaving Han alone. Han would indeed talk to his parents, but he wanted to refrain from confessing his feelings to Xiaofan for the time being. He wanted to examine every possibility, every positive *and* negative outcome, and he didn't want to make Xiaofan a promise that he couldn't keep.

His parents were supposed to arrive at Baoshu tomorrow, so he had to stay away from Xiaofan until then. He didn't trust himself to be near her; he didn't trust himself to resist running up to her and kissing her hard on her sweet lips. But knowing that *she* also had feelings for *him* made him feel hopeful, and he was going to do everything he could to be with the woman he loved.

XIAOFAN ADMIRED THE VIEWS BELOW HER—THE WAVES crashing against the shore, and the ships approaching the harbor that looked like tiny ants swimming through the ocean and struggling to reach dry land—the day before Kyrie's wedding, and she closed her eyes as the breeze slowly brushed against her face and ruffled through her hair. She felt so appreciative for this moment and everything she had right now—her new incredible family, an extraordinary and overly empathic sister, a best friend whom she could share her secrets with, and most importantly, the potential love of her life.

But she couldn't help but wonder what his *true* feelings for her were. Every time she thought they were getting along, he'd disappear for hours after. And they were always meeting by chance, not by choice. Was he avoiding her?

"Men. They're always such an enigma," she whispered to herself and turned to go back inside to get dressed for the big dinner.

"Dinner? What dinner? Why didn't you tell me this sooner?" Han exclaimed to Zhang while he marched from corner to corner in his room. "I'm supposed to be *avoiding* Xiaofan until my parents come, not having dinner with her!"

"Well, it wouldn't *just* be with her. We'll all be there. And you know you can't disappoint Kyrie. She'll never get over it," Zhang told him firmly.

"But what if I accidentally say something that I'm not supposed to? I can't just ignore her if she's sitting right in front of me!"

Zhang groaned. "It is what it is, Han. You can't stop fate's bidding."

Han was hesitant, but then his pacing slowed to a stop. He gave his friend one final look before nodding once. "You're right. Let's do this."

The dinner was held at the back courtyard of the kingdom. The ground was covered with well-trimmed green grass, shadowed by rich willow trees that were in full bloom with luminous yellow flowers dancing in the breeze. A handwoven carpet was spread in the middle of the yard, and a long, thin table was placed over it. There were glass chandeliers hanging from the trees with tiny candles lit upon them, the air was fresh with a fragrance of cherry blossoms flowing through it, and oil lamps were hung on every perch.

Xiuying and Kamari were the first ones to reach the courtyard, followed by Zhang and Han. The two men were left speechless as their eyes gazed over the dinner setup. Both of them were thoroughly impressed by how ravishing and elegant it looked.

Ming and Huiqing walked in next.

"This looks like a fairytale!" Huiqing smiled in awe.

"It sure does," Ming agreed.

When Xiaofan walked in with Kyrie—the guest of honor—Kyrie started to cry at how beautiful everything looked. Zhang gave her a hug while everyone else clapped.

Han, however, couldn't take his eyes off of Xiaofan. His heart started to beat faster with every step she took toward the table. Her hair was curled with her bangs hanging loose, she wore a shimmery lilac dress, her cheeks glowed a baby pink, and he couldn't look away.

Xiaofan sat next to him, and Han struggled with the internal battle between his heart and his mind. He wanted to reach out and touch Xiaofan, but he knew he shouldn't. He held himself back. Instead, he turned toward Zhang and started talking to him, but he could feel Xiaofan's flickering glances on him, and his fingers twitched to reach out and take hers. He clenched them tightly on his lap.

The table was full of cheers as they celebrated

Kyrie's last meal at home. She was always the brightest light in the room, so full of laughter and warmth. The castle wouldn't be the same without her.

But while everyone else cheered, Xiaofan felt a knife piercing through her heart. Kyrie was her friend, her *best* friend. And even though they'd only known each other for a short time, she found her irreplaceable. What would she do without her? Her mind darkened, and she looked for support to her left. Han *did* promise to always support her, be there when she needed it. And yet, Han hadn't looked at her once since she arrived.

Maybe it was all just a misunderstanding, and I misread him, Xiaofan thought as she took a sip from her soup that had now grown cold. They bonded; they had become friends, and maybe... more? *Was it all just my imagination?* He had been so open, so caring, and now... he wouldn't even look at her. She was about to lose her best friend, and now the man she thought she loved left her feeling even more alone.

All she wanted to do was run to her room and hide under her blankets so she wouldn't have to face any of this. But she couldn't. How could she leave Kyrie's final dinner? How could she let down someone who had been like a sister to her since the day she arrived? She couldn't.

Xiuying was worried when she saw Xiaofan's face darken and her body curl inwards. Han's attention was on Zhang, and Kyrie was busy interacting with her parents. She knew Xiaofan probably felt incredibly alone. Xiuying knew the feeling all too well in her past. But this feeling of isolation... it wasn't necessary. It could be avoided.

She knew how much Xiaofan loved Han, but she also knew that Han was in a sticky situation himself. She knew that all he was trying to do was protect Xiaofan by avoiding her until he figured things out, but did she *need* protection? Xiaofan was left in the dark in regards to Han's problem, and because of that, she probably thought something was wrong with *her*. Xiuying shook her head absently. Her sister deserved to know the truth; Han owed her that much.

Zhang had told Xiuying every detail of what Han was going through, and being the caring sister that she was, she was eager to save her younger sister from a heartbreak that didn't need to happen. She needed to speak to Xiaofan after dinner. If Han wouldn't support her now, she would.

A few hours later, dinner came to an end. Kyrie was emotional and wanted to spend time with her parents. Kamari was tired from all the preparations, so she bid farewell and left for her room. Zhang and Han left early to discuss some urgent issues, or so they said. This left the sisters alone. Xiuying opened her mouth to ask Xiaofan if she wanted company, but a servant came into the courtyard and called for her attention. Once Xiuying was finished, she turned back to her sister, but Xiaofan was already gone. She sighed and made her way toward her sister's room.

Xiaofan walked alone back to her room with a

shattered heart. She should've known that Han was too good to be true. She should've known that a prince like him could *never* fall for someone like her. She entered her room and closed the door behind her. She looked at her bed, but her legs failed to carry her there. Instead, she sat on the floor with her head resting on her knees, and she let herself fall apart.

"Why won't he love me?" She sobbed around her wavering voice. After years of being unloved and unsupported at Jinu, and then at the orphanage, she was *sick* of being second. She was *sick* of being ignored.

"All I want is love, but no matter what I do or how hard I try, I can never have it," she whispered into her knees.

Three knocks on her door silenced her. The only person who knocked three times—Xiuying entered to find Xiaofan huddled on the floor. Xiuying slowly walked in, closed the door behind her, lit some candles to conquer the darkness, and then sat on the floor next to her sister.

"What's wrong, Xiaofan?" Xiuying whispered quietly.

"I'm tired," she croaked out, not caring if she looked and sounded like a mess. "I'm tired of being the one to always give up what makes me happy. Why can't Han be mine? Why does he pretend to love me one day, and then doesn't even acknowledge my presence the next? I love him..." The words felt too real, too fragile. But they were out there now. "I have never felt this way for anyone else before. And now that I want him, I can't have him."

Xiaofan sniffled, her tears falling like a river down her red face. Xiuying was done seeing Xiaofan in this state, and each one of her sister's tears felt like a needle stabbing through her own heart. A part of her wanted to share what Han was going through to give Xiaofan some relief, but the other part of her insisted that it was not her story to share. Han was going to talk to Xiaofan sooner or later. She just had to hold out a little longer.

Xiuying breathed and scooted closer, wrapping an arm around her sister's shoulders. Even if this was all the support she could offer right now, she hoped it would be enough. "Xiaofan, there's so much that I cannot say right now, but remember that sometimes people have their reasons. Sometimes they have to choose a harder path to save their loved ones from dismay. So, don't jump to conclusions just yet, okay?"

Xiaofan nodded weakly, and Xiuying's heart squeezed in her chest. She wanted to do more. She wanted to help her sister more. She took a long, steadying breath.

"You are only signing yourself up for heartbreak when you expect, Xiaofan. Expectations come naturally, I understand, but they are always followed by disappointment." Xiuying wiped her sister's tears away with gentle fingers.

Xiaofan looked up at her. "What do you mean? Should I not expect him to love me back after everything that happened between us?" Xiaofan tried to wrap her mind around everything that Xiuying had said, but something tickled her thoughts. There was more to it. "Is there something you're not telling me, Xiuying?"

"Time will tell, Xiaofan. Just be patient," Xiuying said, stroking slow fingers through the ends of Xiaofan's loose strands of hair. "Even if someone loves you, they are always going to disappoint you one way or another. It's just how human beings are. The only love that's never going to disappoint you is the one that stays with you, the one that cannot be lost even with death. So, put your trust in the right place, and everything will fall in line for you, Xiaofan."

Xiaofan's tears slowed, and her lips curled into a small smile as her sister's words soothed her. "How do you always know the right things to say?"

Xiuying chuckled. "It's just something I've learned along the way." Xiuying hugged her tight and breathed in her sister's scent as they held onto each other. "Now get some sleep. It's already late, and Kyrie's big day is tomorrow."

Xiaofan nodded and thanked her sister once more before Xiuying left the room. Xiaofan climbed into bed and closed her eyes, promising herself to not jump to any conclusions before hearing from Han. After what Xiuying had said, she suspected that there was something left unsaid. She would learn what it was in time; she just had to be patient. She would wait for Han. She *had* to.

Han left the dinner with Zhang, but he went straight to his room alone. Dinner was incredibly hard for him. He had to force himself to ignore Xiaofan and was fully aware of how that made her feel. His determination almost crumbled when he saw her curl inwards and stare at her soup in silence halfway through the meal.

He hated himself for listening to his mind, he despised himself for not telling her how gorgeous she looked, he loathed himself for not talking to her, and most of all, he abhorred his existence for not being able to confess his true feelings to her. He was certain that he had lost her.

"Why is this happening to me?!" he screamed. "Am I going to lose the only girl I have ever loved?"

The dinner made him realize how his mind weighed over his heart, and he feared that when the time came to make a decision, he might end up choosing a choice that he'd regret for a lifetime.

His love for Xiaofan was true, but their tale was utterly tragic and filled with uncertainty. Xiaofan was carrying a heart filled with love for Han, while Han was unconsciously caught up in the war that his heart and mind waged against one another.

CHAPTER EIGHT

XIAOFAN WOKE UP THE NEXT MORNING WITH A LITTLE BIT OF hope, ignorant to what was ahead, while Han woke up tired and filled with dread. His parents arrived at the kingdom right after sunrise, but they brought a guest that no one was expecting.

It was Han's future wife! His parents thought the wedding would be a great chance for them to get to know each other, to be introduced together in a formal setting, and to mingle with the royals and allies of this kingdom. They introduced her as his fiancé without any promises being made. And before Han had even gotten a chance to talk to his parents, the entire kingdom seemed to know about his *fiancé*.

Kamari, Kyrie, and Xiuying were startled upon meeting his parents and the princess. *Nobody* expected this to happen, and they feared what Xiaofan would feel. Han's fiancé was a sweetheart at first—beautiful and proper—but after a while, her true nature started to show.

She started throwing tantrums. She didn't get along with Kamari or Kyrie. Sure, she was a princess, and she behaved like one in the worst way possible—she treated people like they were beneath her, and she insulted everyone as if they were peasants.

Her name was Rai, and *pretense* could be defined by her existence. She was a saint in front of Han and Zhang's parents, but behind their backs, she was a living nightmare for everyone around her. She sat next to Han after the parents of both families left and kept a firm grip on his hand. Han felt humiliated and irritated, both feelings visible through his face and body language.

"Oh, Han! I can't believe I'm going to be your wife soon! Girls, guess who the luckiest girl here is—it's Rai!" She laughed. The sound was whiny and grating on Han's ears.

"Who talks about themselves in the third person?" Kyrie whispered to Xiaofan.

"I don't like her," Kamari mumbled to the others while smiling at Rai and sipping her tea.

Xiaofan's face was pale, and she didn't say a word

from the moment she joined them for brunch. After all the support that Xiuying had offered her the night before and the hope that she had awoken with that morning, she was fighting back tears, vowing not to cry in front of everyone.

But how unlucky was Han?! He sat across the table from Xiaofan, but he couldn't do *anything* to ease her noticeable distress without turning Rai into a monster. But it wasn't Rai or his parents or the situation that bothered him the most. What he hated most was that *he* was the reason behind Xiaofan's sorrow.

Rai continued bragging about all her riches, even if no one was paying her any attention. The other girls all rolled their eyes and constantly sipped from their cups to avoid talking to her.

"What an egotistical, self-centered b—witch!" Kamari whispered while Rai went on and on about her wealth.

"Agree," Kyrie mumbled. "Han deserves better." Kyrie reached over and squeezed Xiaofan's hand under the table, giving her friend an encouraging look. But Xiaofan's smile wobbled with effort.

"I have to go." Xiaofan pushed herself up from her seat.

"What? Where?" Kyrie's smile plummeted.

"I have a few lectures to go through before the wedding. Just some work from the university. But I'll be back before the ceremony!" Xiaofan lied and abruptly turned to leave.

Xiuying tried to go after her, but Zhang held onto

her hand. "Let her be. She needs to do this alone," he said in a low voice.

"There goes the bookworm," Rai mocked, rolling her eyes in annoyance. "There's no point in reading books; it's all just fantasy. What a waste of time and money! I'd rather be doing better things—like shopping." Rai snorted, looking to Han for approval.

But Han had enough. He yanked his hand out of Rai's grasp and moved to follow Xiaofan.

"Han! Where are you going?" Rai called.

Han ignored her as he left them all behind.

He couldn't wrap his mind around what had happened. Things had blown *way* out of proportion, and now it was going to be even harder to talk to his parents. But he was determined. He would *never* marry Rai, not after seeing her true nature. He was going to fight for Xiaofan, and he would accept no one else.

He rushed toward his parents' room to have the conversation that he had been avoiding. It was now or never.

"There's our son! Oh, I have been *dying* to see your face. We saw each other for such a short time at brunch," his mother greeted him with a long hug.

"Our boy! Becoming a man *and* a king," his father added, patting him on the back.

"I was waiting for you both as well," Han said, his body tense. "But as happy as I am to see you both, I don't appreciate Rai being here."

His father's joy melted away almost instantly as he looked at his son with stale eyes. This was the first time in his life that Han had objected to a decision they made.

"What do you mean? We thought you would be happy to see her. You would get a chance to know her and show her off to our allies," his mother said, her smile dipping, too.

But Han couldn't hide his true feelings any longer. "I have seen enough of her, and I do *not* want to marry her. Please send her back," Han said firmly. "I've made no commitments to her, and I do not intend to move forward with engaging her."

His father's eyes widened, and the lines on his forehead deepened. "You are crossing a line, Han. We gave our word to her parents. They have entrusted her to us and sent her here so that she could meet you. I will *not* tolerate *anyone* going against my decision."

"If they trusted you so much, then why is there an army of soldiers here with her, Father? But like I said, I am *not* going to marry her, and that's final," Han stated.

His mother stared at him in a state of shock. She had never seen Han so determined to stand up against something that they had decided for him. He was usually so eager to please them.

"Why are you suddenly so against this union? Is there someone else whom you would like to consider?" his mother asked.

Han hung his head; his eyes wandered along the floor, and his feet tapped an anxious rhythm. "There is."

His parents both looked at each other, and then they looked at him. He had never mentioned a girl before.

"Who is it?" his mother murmured.

"It's Xiaofan," Han said firmly. Every trace of hesitation and doubt dissipated as he confessed what was in his heart all along. "I love her. I cannot see my life with anyone else but her."

It felt like a weight had been lifted from Han's chest. Everything was brighter, the air was easier to breathe, and a warmth in his chest fluttered. Han's mother could see the affection that he had for Xiaofan when he spoke about her, and she smiled. But before she could say anything else, his father put his foot down.

"I will *not* tolerate such nonsense. Rai is the *perfect* match for you, and her presence will benefit you and our kingdom. If you refuse to marry her, you will have to walk away from us as well."

Han stared at his father in disbelief. After years of obeying every single one of his decisions, *this* was how his father reacted when Han asked to make his own for once—a decision that impacted both his future *and* his happiness. He gritted his teeth and straightened as he met his father's gaze.

"I am *not* going to marry Rai, and I am *not* going to walk away from my own parents," he said firmly. "There's more to life than power and wealth, Father. I pray that you understand that before you lose those who are important to you."

His father stared at him with a crimson face, full of rage and ready to explode. But Han didn't wait for his response. He turned and left the room with his spine still straight and his pride intact. He felt powerful. He felt free. He felt like he had been taken out of captivity, and finally, he would be able to confess his true feelings to Xiaofan... despite what his parents wished for him. His heart won over his mind this time, and the internal battle quieted. He knew there would be more to discuss later with his parents, but for now, he wanted to let his heart lead him.

XIAOFAN HAD WALKED TO BRUNCH THAT MORNING IN HOPES that Han would talk to her, explain what had been going through his mind, and even if Han didn't reach out, she was going to talk to him anyway. But what happened was beyond anything that she had ever expected.

Han was engaged, and now everything made sense —why he'd been ignoring her. Maybe she was right after all, this was all just a fairytale.

She was so naïve! How could she even *think* that a *prince* could ever love her? All her feelings had been one-sided, and she was lying to herself to think that Han wanted to be with her also.

After walking out of brunch, Xiaofan went straight to her room and cried until her eyes were swollen.

"Horrible, isn't it?" she asked herself. "Being in

love makes you vulnerable. It opens your heart to someone, and then when you're hopeful and happy, it slashes it in two." She chuckled to herself sinisterly.

Her relationship with Han would *just* be as *friends*. But it wasn't Han's fault; it was all on her. And she could cry and sulk later when she had time to pity herself, but she knew she had to gather her emotions and be her best self for Kyrie's wedding. But that alone felt impossible in this moment.

She needed to relieve her mind and vanish her thoughts, so she decided to write them down. She remembered Xiuying telling her once that writing about her feelings helped her get them out of her head and onto paper. Xiaofan couldn't talk to Han about her feelings. Maybe *this* was the only way to expose everything to him.

Han,

It's time I move on. It's time I get out of the perfect world that I have created in my head for us. You have been such a good friend to me, but I mistook that for something more.

I thought we had something, felt something for each other. I certainly did for you. But I was a fool to think that you'd ever want a nobody like me. You're engaged to a princess, even if I do think you deserve better, but now I realize that better doesn't mean me.

I love you, Han, but you are not mine.

I'll never forget you, but I have to move on.

Xiaofan

She knew she had fallen for him, but the intensity

increased as she wrote it down. She went to fold the letter, but Kyrie suddenly came bursting into her room.

"I know you're not in the right headspace right now, Xiaofan, but I *really* need you."

"It's your big day, Kyrie. Anything for you." She placed the letter on her desk and followed Kyrie out of the room and down the hall.

Han was eager to see Xiaofan. He wanted to tell her everything—the reason why he had to ignore her and stay away from her—and now he couldn't hold himself back from her anymore. He made his way to her room in hopes that he could clear everything up.

He rounded the corner of the hall and slowed as he approached her room. The door was cracked open. He knocked twice but heard no answer, so he peeked his head through the crack. No one was inside. He stepped into the empty room and looked for clues as to where Xiaofan could have gone. As he turned around, his eyes caught his name on a piece of paper that sat on her desk.

"She *did* love me," he whispered as he read her letter. "All this time, she just wanted to be with me, and I've done nothing but make it all worse. X-Xiao-fan, I love you, too."

Xiaofan was moving on. After everything that had happened between them and the mishap with Rai, she was going to force herself forward *without* him. He picked up the ink quill and a blank piece of paper, and he sat down to write.

Xiaofan,

I know you don't think I like you as more than just a friend, but I do. I love you, and I can only imagine my future with you, not Rai, not anyone else. I'm so sorry for making you think otherwise as I have loved you since the day we first met.

I hope you don't move on. I hope that one day, we can finally be together because we deserve to be together. You will always have my heart, and if I were to ever get married, it would be with you.

Han paused—he only had one more chance to make this right. He had to try one more time.

I'll wait for you at midnight by the staircase outside your room, and if you decide not to come, then I promise to leave you alone forever.

With love,

Han

He folded the note and scrawled her name across the top before placing it on her desk. Then he walked away.

Xiaofan, on the other hand, was busy helping Kyrie with her wedding gown. Kyrie wore a traditional qipao with a complimenting hairstyle. She looked divine, as usual.

"You're the prettiest bride I have ever seen," Xiaofan praised her as she handed over a bouquet of white and red roses.

"You don't look too bad yourself." Kyrie grinned before softening her smile. "Han will lose his mind seeing you like this."

Xiaofan chuckled dryly. "I am probably the *last* person he's going to pay attention to."

Kyrie huffed, not even trying to hide her distaste. "I hope Rotten Rai falls off a cliff. I swear, I *cannot* tolerate her! She keeps blabbering about herself. Ugh!"

Xiaofan chuckled at her friend's forwardness, and Kamari walked into the dressing room just in time to catch the end of Kyrie's curse.

"That's what we're calling her? Rotten Rai?" She laughed, but her eyes glowed once she caught sight of Kyrie. "I can't believe you're getting married! You can still change your mind; there's still time," she added, receiving a playful push from her sister.

"Please, I would do this a thousand times over for my husband!" Kyrie giggled.

"Husband-to-be," Kamari corrected.

"Soon enough!" Kyrie grinned, posing in front of the mirror.

Kamari and Xiaofan laughed as they finished helping Kyrie get ready. The wedding ceremony would start soon enough, and there was no time to think about anything else.

CHAPTER NINE

"The groom's here. We have to leave," Xiuying announced as she walked into the room, and Kyrie started jumping in excitement.

"Finally!" she screamed.

Zhang and Ming walked Kyrie down the aisle when the ceremony began, surrounded by friends and family. It was a scenic view. The venue was filled with lavender flowers, chandeliers with candles lit atop them, and oil lamps in every other corner. The color combination of off-white and different shades of purple was a pleasing sight for all eyes.

Xiaofan matched the aesthetic with a dark purple robe that had bell sleeves and lavender flowers embroidered onto it. She wore her hair down with blossoms pinned in the back and finished off the look with a maroon lip balm.

Han was standing in front of Xiaofan, and he kept glancing at her every now and then. Xiaofan would look away and try to refrain from any eye contact or exchanging smiles. He looked so incredibly handsome in his elegant black robe.

The wedding ceremony ended sooner than Xiaofan was prepared for. Once everyone started clapping and cheering, Xiaofan realized with dread that it was time. Her best friend was going to leave her. Saying goodbye had never been this hard for Xiaofan, but Kyrie had given her many firsts in her life. She would never forget her, *never*. As she watched Kyrie ride away with her new husband, a hole was left in her heart. She felt like she had now lost the two most important people in her life. Ming and Zhang were right. Kyrie *was* the heart of the kingdom, and a certain kind of silence took over the moment she left.

"Are you okay?" Xiuying stepped beside her and asked.

Xiaofan shook her head and started to walk toward her room.

"I understand that this has been a hard day for you," Xiuying started slowly as she walked beside her sister.

Xiaofan paused before replying, "Life seems to get harder every day."

Xiuying worried about her sister's numbness, her distance. She wanted to console her, but she had no words to say. She knew all too well how she felt. "It's not all bad," she tried. "I'm always here if you ever need to talk about anything."

Xiaofan barely nodded as she entered her room. Xiuying didn't want to leave her alone, but there was nothing else that she could do right now. Her sister needed space and time alone to decompress.

Inside her room alone, Xiaofan removed the flowers from her hair and changed into her nightgown. She sat down in front of the mirror, thinking that the day had passed by in less than a blink. She glanced over her reflection, and before she knew it, she started to cry again. Her nose turned red, her eyes were already swollen, and tears were rapidly rolling down her cheeks. She choked on a shallow, thick breaths raking her body with trembling shakes.

Xiaofan felt alone despite having people around who cared about her. She noticed how close Xiuying was to Zhang, how close Kyrie was to her husband, and how close Ming and Huiqing were to each other. Just like at the orphanage, everyone had found their missing half except for her.

She wanted her happy ending, too. She wanted to find *her* missing half.

She looked up and stared at her own reflection through blurry eyes. She couldn't recognize herself, but at the same time, she felt seen. Maybe *that* was the reason why she often cried in front of the mirror... because she wanted to be seen, heard, and understood.

Maybe.

The weather soon changed. The night sky was covered with dark rumbling clouds, and the winds were roaring, causing the windows to slam open and shut. Xiaofan stood up to close the windows when she saw the sky burst with light as a lightning bolt ripped through the darkness, with a loud thunder echoing it moments later. She closed the window and turned around to light the oil lamp sitting on her desk.

The room was now a bit brighter than before. The flame of the lamp flickered as light breezes of wind crossed the room. That's when she noticed the letter. She moved to grab it and found her initials scrawled across the top of it. She quickly unfolded it, and her eyes started to read the curly handwriting. Word after word, she read and realized how wrong she had been. He was waiting for her; he *promised* he would wait for her. She looked outside the window and peered out into the dark. It had to be past midnight. Was it too late?

Overwhelmed by emotions, she started to feel her hands grow hot, and after a few seconds, the paper that she held in her hands began to slowly burn. Her emotions were aligning with her magical power... just as they had on the streets outside her orphanage.

"I can't let him go. I can't let him go!" she repeated to herself and scurried toward the door.

She ran as fast as she could, her breaths heavy and aching in her lungs as she pushed onward. The thunder was growing louder as the night went on, and the sky was pouring like it hadn't rained in months.

What if he left?

She grabbed a lantern and found her way through the darkness. She rushed toward the staircase, and the ground was soaked with fiery puddles as she held her light over them. She heaved a deep breath through her mouth as she stopped at the top step. She looked around but saw no one.

Am I too late?

Is he gone forever?

Her thoughts were caving into her, when suddenly, she heard a familiar voice.

"I didn't think you'd come," Han whispered with relief in his voice as he stepped around the corner and stopped just shy of the steps.

Xiaofan looked at him, warmth radiating through her even in the wet cold that was surrounding her. "I thought I was too late."

Han took a few steps toward her. "I'll *always* wait for you." He wrapped his arms around her waist and pulled her closer to him before leaning his head toward her and kissing her passionately on the lips. He could feel his heart flutter as Xiaofan kissed him back, and he never wanted this moment to end. "I love you, Xiaofan. I don't know what our future holds, but I want you to know that the love I have for you is real, and I will fight for us no matter what happens."

Xiaofan was speechless, but somehow she squeaked out, "Why?"

Han didn't hesitate. "Because you deserve it. You are worth it. And I will endure any torture in the world if it means I can spend the rest of my days with you." Han paused as they walked toward a nearby shed to sit down. He scooted closer as they huddled together to stay warm. Han's breath was hot, and his warmth was welcoming, but he wasn't done.

"I want to be honest with you, Xiaofan." She braced herself for what he was about to say. "My parents are against us. They don't want us to be together; they want me to be with Rai, but my heart disagrees. And the only reason why I've been avoiding you is because I don't know how to choose—how to choose between you and my parents."

Xiaofan listened, feeling an ounce of guilt because she felt like she was tearing his family apart. Parents were something that she didn't really have growing up, and she didn't like that Han had decided to go against his—for her, nonetheless. But she stayed silent and kept her worries to herself.

Han kept her hand firmly in his own, and after a while, he realized that her grip was warm... warmer than usual.

"Are you sick?" he asked.

Xiaofan froze.

"Is everything okay?" Han asked again.

"I have something to tell you, and it might make you see me in a different way."

Han chuckled nervously and rubbed the back of his neck. "I can assure you that'll never happen. Even if you killed someone, I can't promise you that I won't still love you."

Xiaofan took a deep breath as she focused her eyes on the ground before her. The raindrops landing in front of her soothed her nerves.

"My blood family is... different. We all have magical powers, given to us when we were born. Xiuying can control plants, mostly. And I can control fire and wind. My emotions channel them. I'm still learning how to use my magic, but my hands tend to grow warm whenever I feel... love." She looked down at their intertwined fingers.

"You love me?" Han blushed.

"I do, and I don't think I'll ever stop," Xiaofan whispered.

"Well, you were right about one thing."

"What is it?"

"I *do* see you in a different way."

Xiaofan felt her face turn red with shame, and she started to get up and leave when Han pulled her back down and into his arms.

"Your power makes you even more special. How can I ever let someone as amazing as you go?" He smirked and pressed his lips against hers.

She could feel her heart beating faster and faster against her chest, her body turning warmer and warmer, and she was pressing so hard against him that she felt like her body was going to absorb right into his.

Han slid one of his hands slowly under her nightgown, and the skin-to-skin contact made Xiaofan's body shiver with a sensation that she'd never felt before. She kissed him even harder as he gently made his way up her body... before suddenly stopping and whispering into her ear.

"I want you, Xiaofan. I really do. But not yet, not until I figure out this mess."

"Oh..."

"Please don't think I'm pushing you away. I've only been dreaming about this moment ever since I first laid eyes on you, but it's not right to do it like this. I have to do it the right way." He paused. "Wait for me. Please? I promise you that this will all work out. I love you with all my heart, and you have my word that we *will* be together."

"I will wait for you." She smiled, and they kissed once more before he walked her back to her room and tucked her into bed.

Xiaofan woke up just mere hours later to a sun ray touching her face. She felt different today, better—happier. Finally, she had someone she could call hers, and that someone was Han. He was her happy ending, and she couldn't even begin to think of someone better.

Han's parents were going to stay at Baoshu over the next three days, and Xiaofan knew that those three days would decide her fate with Han. However, she tried not to let it bother her too much. He had promised her that he'd be with her no matter what, and she knew she had to trust him.

Xiaofan threw on her robe and wrapped a purple lavender ribbon around her hair, ready to head to the university. On her way out, she stopped by her sister's room.

"Finally drag yourself out of bed?" Xiuying asked in a teasing tone. "I stopped by earlier, and you were fast asleep. Did you stay up late?"

Xiaofan blushed. "Sort of. Can we meet up for tea later? I want to tell you something."

"Of course! Anything for my baby sister. We can even talk now if you want."

"No, no, you have a lot to do. I don't want to be a burden, and besides, I'm headed to the university."

"Okay... if you're sure. I'll see you tonight, then." Xiuying hugged her, and Xiaofan left.

Xiaofan went straight to the library when she arrived, eager to find the book that all her classmates had been talking about—*Dream of the Red Chamber*. This particular Chinese literature comprised of realism and romance, psychological motivation and supernatural occurrences, all things that she could relate to. And she quickly found herself invested in the pages.

After a few hours, she heard someone take a seat in front of her. She noticed the movement, but kept her head buried in the book until she finished the last paragraph of her current chapter.

She looked up to see Han sitting in front of her, holding a book of poetry in his hands.

"*This* is what I love about you. You are so passionate about the things you choose to read and study." Han grinned.

"Good to see you, too." Xiaofan chuckled.

"Why do you always sit in the corner? It took me almost ten minutes to find you. There's no one else here... if you haven't noticed," Han said as he waved his hands around at the empty tables.

"That is *exactly* why I sit here."

"Wait—you *don't* want me to find you?" Han teased.

"No, I just don't want *others* to find me."

"Understandable." He shrugged. "But I don't like it."

Xiaofan shook her head at him before glancing at his own book. "What are you reading?"

"You mean, what am I going to read to *you*? Poetry. *Romance*."

Xiaofan laughed, but Han was having none of it. He gently nudged her book aside.

"Take a break from that. I'll read to you," he said with a smirk.

"Okay, fine." Xiaofan submitted but felt the need to add, "But you can't read out loud. It's a library."

"Yeah, but you're the only human here, Xiaofan." Han laughed.

The poem was about a requited love that was still incomplete, and that made Han wonder if his own story was going to be fully complete one day. He had *his* requited love, and she wanted to stay by his side, too, but their future was undetermined.

Xiaofan was moved by the words that came out of Han. The pauses and the way that he spoke made her saw him as a true poet, portraying the strong emotions that only a lover could show.

The two of them settled together in silence, reading from their books and peeking small glimpses and smiles at each other when their love bubbled over. As the hours ticked by, and the light outside the windows dimmed, Xiaofan set down her book with a sigh.

"I should leave. I have to meet Xiuying for tea, and it's almost sunset," she said.

"Of course," Han replied and escorted her toward her carriage. But as they walked, his mind and his gaze lingered on her.

Every time he saw Xiaofan, every second he spent with her, made him realize how much he wanted her to be his queen, how much he wanted to spend every second of his life with her. But at the same time, he wanted acceptance from his parents, and he couldn't have one without the other. He had to try to talk some sense into his parents again today, with hopes that they would welcome Xiaofan with open arms, and for once, listen to what Han wanted.

Xiaofan reached the castle to find Xiuying waiting for her on the grand terrace, admiring the heavenly view. She hurried her way upstairs and rushed to meet her sister.

"I'm here!" Xiaofan sang cheerfully as she stepped onto the terrace.

"Welcome back." Xiuying grinned, giving her a hug. "Someone's in a good mood."

Xiaofan couldn't stop her smile.

"Oh, Kamari will be joining us, too. I hope that's not a problem," Xiuying added.

"Not a problem at all," Xiaofan replied and grabbed one of the moon cakes that were on the table between them. "And thanks for remembering the moon cakes."

"Always," Xiuying replied, and then she asked, "So?"

Xiaofan looked at her in bewilderment before repeating with a giggle, "So?"

"What did you want to discuss? And what changed since last night? You were so devastated after our last conversation."

Xiaofan paused, floundering to find a way to explain what exactly had ensued. Because even after Han had confessed his feelings for her, their future was still highly uncertain, and she didn't know what would become of their story. After staying silent and taking into consideration the choice of words, Xiaofan spoke.

"I met up with Han last night. He left a note on my desk, confessing his feelings and assuring me that he wasn't actually engaged. We saw each other, and he explained his side of the story—what his parents had planned for him, and how he only wants to be with me. He loves me, Sister, and I love him back. I want to give our story a chance to come true."

Xiuying wanted to be happy for her sister, but instead, she was worried. She had been around Han's parents for long enough to know that his parents would *never* accept Xiaofan, despite how much love Han had for her. And they would forever despise Xiaofan for turning their son against them. But then again, Xiaofan was so happy. How could she take that away from her?

"I'm glad he feels the same way about you, Xiaofan. Nothing will make me happier than seeing you find love. But his parents are difficult; they are not going to just give up on their decision that easily."

"I know. But Han and I can win them over; I know we can!" Xiaofan cheered.

"I hope you do." Xiuying faked a smile, but deep down, she feared that Xiaofan was only setting herself up for disappointment.

Kamari came rushing in just seconds later, huffing and puffing from all the stress of carrying the kingdom ever since Kyrie left.

"You need a break, Kamari. I think you're over-working yourself," Xiaofan said.

"I will... *after* the charity gala," Kamari replied.

"It's just two days away," Xiuying added. "I almost forgot!"

"What's it about?" Xiaofan asked.

Kamari took a deep breath before passionately replying, "Discount Day—a day where shops can offer to sell their products at low, low prices to help out those who can't afford them. We do this every quarter. Everyone from the community volunteers and donates—they all look forward to helping out. That's why I work so hard to make it a success every year."

"Can I volunteer to help out?" Normally, Xiaofan wouldn't be into charity, but she was so in love that she wanted to help everyone else feel the same happiness that she did.

"Of course, you can," Kamari replied, reaching forward to grab her cup. "This has gotten so cold."

"Don't worry." Xiaofan smiled, holding out her hand. "Give it to me."

Kamari was confused, and so was Xiuying. "No, I'll get it reheated by the maid. You don't have to do it for me, Xiaofan."

"Trust me," Xiaofan insisted.

Kamari raised a brow before slowly setting down the cup in her hand. Xiaofan placed both of her palms around the cup and closed her eyes. Her hands started to grow warmer and warmer by the second, and within a minute, vapor started to flow from its surface. Xiuying and Kamari looked at each other in shock.

"Here." Xiaofan passed the cup back to Kamari. When Kamari touched it, it was burning hot. She set it back down with a hiss.

"How did you do this?" Xiuying asked.

"My power. I can control fire and wind with my emotions."

"That's amazing!" Kamari exclaimed.

Xiuying felt tears of happiness glittering at the corners of her eyes. She remembered when she first discovered her own power. That moment meant a lot to her, and she was proud of Xiaofan for showing it to her and Kamari.

"I'm so proud of you," Xiuying whispered with teary eyes, and she leaned in to give Xiaofan a hug.

"Now I miss Kyrie even more!" Kamari whined, and then joined their happy embrace.

While Xiaofan's heart was filled with optimism, Han's essence was getting obscured by shadows of doubt. As time passed, he was coming to the realization that he had taken his parents a little too lightly. He knew it wasn't going to be easy, and with all the uncertainty, he was only certain about one thing. In the end, he would have to make a choice—give up on one and choose the other.

After escorting Xiaofan, he, too, went back to the

castle, and on his way, he prepared himself for a conversation that he was *not* looking forward to. On his way inside, he caught a glimpse of Xiaofan laughing alongside Xiuying and Kamari on the grand terrace. The sight of her gave him the strength to fight harder. He walked toward the royal guest room—where his parents were staying—and knocked on the door. The door opened, and his mother welcomed him.

"It feels like I haven't seen you in an eternity, my son," she cooed. "Come in, come in!" She urged Han inside as she closed the door behind him.

His father was at the study desk, reading a manuscript.

"How are you, Father?" Han asked.

"My answer depends on your decision, my son. Has your mind come to its senses?" He pushed himself up, walked toward the center of the room, and sat down on a wooden chair while offering Han a seat next to him.

"I have not changed my decision. I want to marry Xiaofan," Han replied, looking down at the ground.

"I'm afraid that is not possible. We will *not* let an orphan become a part of our legacy, our kingdom. My ancestors deserve better," his father declared.

"And what about your son? What about what I want?" Han pushed.

"You know it as well as I do. Royals have to make compromises for their legacy. We have to choose carefully, and I will *not* let you make this mistake. I will *not* let you ruin what we have built. Your immature love affair will *die* in a few days."

"It's *not* an immature love affair," Han whispered, shaking his head in disagreement.

"What was that?" his father questioned.

"I said, it's *not* an immature love affair," Han repeated while looking directly into his father's eyes. "I want her to be by my side... as my wife."

His father paused, glaring at his son before speaking, "I will *not* tolerate this. I will *not* let our only son marry a girl without an identity. This is where this conversation ends, and you make a choice. Either you listen to us and stay connected to our family, become the future of our kingdom, and inherit everything, or you choose that... orphan and forget that you ever belonged to royalty."

His father was stiff. His eyes were red with anger as he stared at his only son. Han was quiet—thoughtful. He let out a slow sigh and pushed himself out of the chair.

"Okay," he said.

"Okay, you'll forget that girl?"

Han looked at his father with a level gaze. "There is no place for me in a kingdom that does not understand me."

Han's mother had been listening to the argument silently, but when Han uttered the words that she was dreading, she could not believe her ears. "Are you—are you *leaving* your parents for a... g-girl?" she stammered with her eyes leaking thick tears.

Han looked at her, but had no words to answer her question. He wanted to console her, but what could he do? Before he could respond, his mother fainted and fell to the ground. Han and his father rushed forward.

“Look what you did! You still have time—change your decision!” his father shouted while holding his mother in his arms.

Han didn’t know what to say, not when his mother was pale and fragile on the ground. It seemed that now, he didn’t have much of a choice.

CHAPTER TEN

HAN SPENT THE REST OF THE NIGHT WITH HIS MOTHER, assuring her that he was going to stay by her side, that he was not going to leave her.

Xiuying visited often as it was her responsibility to keep the guests at ease, and she saw everything. She saw the story unfold, how Han's mother was keeping him close, and she realized that Xiaofan had lost what had just begun. She could see the sadness in Han's eyes, the sorrow of the choice he had to make. She wondered why Han and Xiaofan were being put through a trial by faith.

While the entire kingdom was busy taking care of the royal guests, Xiaofan was in her room studying, oblivious to what had happened and how her life had just changed within a few hours. Xiuying told everyone not to tell Xiaofan about the incident. She asked Han to do it himself instead, whenever his mother fell asleep.

On the other hand, Han's father felt like he had won a war. He believed that this was his triumph. His son would now marry the girl of his choice. He knew that deep down, Han was glad that this happened, so he could keep the legacy of his kingdom alive!

He made his way over to Xiaofan's room, eager to break the news to her. He wanted to see the look in her eyes when he told her that Han would *never* marry her. And it was going to be *delicious.*

"I'm not here to greet you," he started when she opened the door, a stern look on his face. "I am here to inform you that you have brought great distress to our family. Because of you, my wife's health is suffering. We are *never* going to accept you, never. And we will *never* allow Han to marry you. If he does, he'll always blame you for causing him to go against his own family. Think wisely, my child. You are not living in a fairytale."

Xiaofan shook her head, looking down at the floor in despair. Han's father left the room and closed the door behind him without another word. Xiaofan sat on her bed and wrapped a blanket around her. Her mind was too numb to think about what had just happened. She cried and cried until her sheets were covered with tears. A strong headache took over her mind as she fell asleep.

SHE WOKE UP THE NEXT DAY WITH A HEAVY HEART AND swollen eyes. The words of Han's father were clear in her mind, but she couldn't understand if the whole thing was a figment of her imagination or not. She got out of bed and splashed cold water onto her face to bring herself back to life, but she couldn't feel anything at all. She was numb, her thoughts quiet. All she knew was that she had to leave the castle and go to the library, a place where she could escape the harsh realities of her life.

She threw on her robe and tied her hair into a braid. Her eyes were still swollen and a little red, but she ignored them. On her way, she realized how lonely she was, surrounded by so many people but still had no one. She knew she had to deal with her emotions; there was no point in running anymore. It was going to catch up to her one way or another.

When she walked in, she saw Han. His eyes looked tired and red. He kept rubbing his hands together as his eyes found everything but Xiaofan. She took a shuddering breath.

"It's alright, I understand," she whispered as tears started to roll down her cheeks.

"You know?" Han looked up at her.

"Yes, your father," she replied, but then stopped short.

"My father?" he repeated. "What did he say?"

She knew it wouldn't change anything, but she told him anyway. "He came to my room yesterday and told me what happened. And I agree with him—I will stay away from you. I love you, Han, but I can't be the reason for separating you from your family."

Han looked at her in disbelief. How could his father do that to him? Especially after he agreed to let Xiaofan go. "After I told them that I choose you, my mother fainted. My father basically forced me to reconsider or risk losing my mother forever. I had no other choice, Xiaofan. I can never forgive myself if my mother dies because of me. But believe me, I wanted to choose you; I really did." He shook his head. "Maybe we're just not meant to be together."

"That's not true, Han."

"I don't know what's true anymore, Xiaofan. I thought I would fight for us, and everything would turn out fine," Han said, seemingly disappointed in himself. "I'm sorry."

"I guess this is goodbye," Xiaofan said in a low, shattered voice and walked away without hearing what Han had to say. She couldn't give herself any more reason to believe in their false future.

"I will never forget us. I will miss you, Xiaofan, for the rest of my life," Han whispered to himself as he watched her walk away.

Xiaofan reached the castle and went straight to her

room. Her eyes were filled with tears again, and as soon as she got there, she found Xiuying waiting for her. Seeing her sister sitting on her bed with her eyes locked on the door, Xiaofan started to cry even more. She ran toward Xiuying, sat down beside her on the bed, and sobbed like she never had before.

Xiuying tried to console her, but she was out of words that could make Xiaofan feel better. The kind of heartbreak that Xiaofan was feeling was unknown to Xiuying. It was distinct and extreme. Life had taken away so much from her sister that there were no hopes left in her for her future.

"I had to let him go. I had to love him enough to let him go," Xiaofan whispered. "And now I don't know how I will survive, how I will live without him being around me." Xiaofan sniffled before adding, "I don't think I will ever love anyone the same way ever again."

Xiuying's heart sank while listening to her sister explain her feelings. She had to say something, so she gathered all the strength inside her.

"You're right, Xiaofan. You'll never feel the same love toward another person that you did toward Han, but that doesn't mean you'll never find love again, just a different kind of love. And when you do, you won't even remember why you were so heartbroken. You *will* love again, Sister. I promise." Xiuying paused as she gathered her thoughts. "I know Han had a big impact on you. He loved you for who you are, and now that he's gone, you feel incomplete. But know that he's not the only one who loves you for you; we all do."

Xiaofan understood every word, and it all made sense to her, but saying goodbye to Han was harder and harder to forget. She knew that what they had was over even *before* saying goodbye. All the dreams that she shared with him were shattered and broken into invisible pieces.

"I never want to forget him," Xiaofan muttered.

"You won't forget him. He will always be in your heart," Xiuying assured her. She wiped the tears from Xiaofan's face and helped her stand on her own feet. "You are going to get through this."

Xiaofan nodded.

"Now, try to get some sleep." She helped Xiaofan tuck herself into bed and stayed by her side as she tried to fall asleep.

"Thank you," Xiaofan said. "For always being there for me."

"Always, Xiaofan. I have waited my entire life to be there for you, and I will never miss a chance to help you. I will never let you feel like you are alone."

"You are my home," Xiaofan whispered.

"And you are mine."

Xiaofan woke up to birds chirping by her room's window. The weather was gloomy, the clouds had covered the sky, and the oil lamps were still lit. Xiuying brought in breakfast for her.

"Han and his family are leaving today. I will have to bid them farewell as per kingdom tradition, but you don't have to be there if you don't want to," Xiuying said.

"I'll stay here," Xiaofan muttered.

"Are you sure?" Xiuying asked.

"Yes, we already said our goodbyes," Xiaofan whispered.

"Okay. I will be back after they leave." Xiuying turned around and left the room.

As soon as she was gone, Xiaofan's eyes teared up. She wanted to see him one last time, hear his voice one last time, but she knew that if she went, she would fall apart once again, and she could *not* put herself through the same heartbreak twice. It was best if she started focusing on those she had taken for granted over the past few weeks—her sister, Kyrie, Kamari. They were always there for her, and she had to pull herself out of her own head and return the favor.

AFTER XIAOFAN WALKED OUT, HAN COULD HARDLY GATHER the courage to stand up and leave. If he left, it would mean that everything they had was gone, but what's the point of staying behind? Xiaofan herself had told him to leave, and that they had no future. What was he still trying to prove?

"There's no hope left," Han muttered. "I will have to live without her. She said her farewell. It's over now." Han sighed.

"It will get better with time. You did what had to be done; you saved your mother, Han. Don't be so hard on yourself." Zhang patted his shoulder, and then they stayed silent. Zhang didn't say much to Han, but he had to try one last time to make this all right. He was going to talk to Han's father.

The next day, Han saw the dusk turn into dawn, the colors of the sky change. Han had stayed up all night by the staircase. He sat alone, reliving the memories that he had with Xiaofan. He was never going to see her again, but he hoped he would get a glimpse of her before he left this castle forever.

Zhang took Han's father for a walk and explained what he had coming ahead. "The things I am going to say might offend you, might hurt you, but trust me, I am only looking out for you when I say this. You are not prepared for what is ahead. You might think that you are taking Han with you, and that he is leaving his choice behind, but you are wrong. He is always going to resent you for this. And when he is crowned king in the next few months, I fear what he will do as revenge. People change when they have power; you know that better than me. If I were you, I'd be careful."

The bell sounded, and it was time for Han's family to leave. The ships were ready to set sail, and everyone from the royal family gathered at the main entrance to bid them farewell. Han's parents arrived, and they thanked everyone for the hospitality before boarding their carriage. Zhang was hopeful that something might change after the conversation he had with Han's father, but he saw no progress.

"See you soon," Zhang told Han and reached out his hand.

"Soon," Han replied, shaking it. He looked around, hoping he would see Xiaofan.

"She's not coming," Xiuying said, noticing Han's eyes. "Take care of yourself."

Han shook his head. "Take care of her for me."

Xiuying nodded, and Han left. Their carriage left for the harbor, and so did Zhang's hope that Han's father would change his mind.

Han had grown mute when he reached the harbor. He replied with simple, one-word answers and nothing more. His behavior reminded his father of what Zhang had said. Han's mother noticed, and she blamed her husband's stubbornness.

"You are making a mistake. This will only push him away," she whispered to her husband.

"Is everything loaded?" Han's father asked his son.

"Yes, we leave in ten minutes," Han answered.

His father glanced at Han once more. He saw the despair, the grief, and the spite growing inside of him. He groaned. Zhang was right, and there was *nothing* he could do about it. "Then you should get off," he said before he could stop himself.

Han's eyes flared at him. "What do you mean?"

"I made a mistake, and I don't want you to resent me. I don't want to be the reason for your unhappiness. Xiaofan loves you. I realized that when she agreed to let you go because she wanted our family to stay together. She wanted you to be with your parents. I should have understood this then, but it is not too late. Find her, and ask for her hand in marriage."

Han could not believe his ears, but he quickly stepped off the ship. "Thank you, Father." He beamed and turned to his mother. "Are you okay with Xiaofan joining our family?"

She nodded with a gentle smile of her own. "Yes, I've always liked her. She deserves you, and you deserve her. Now go to her."

Han gave his parents a long hug before running toward the castle to reclaim his missing piece.

This was his life—his future—and he *refused* to spend one more moment of it without Xiaofan by his side.

To be continued...

ABOUT THE AUTHOR

Viola Tempest is a dystopian fantasy and paranormal romance author who yearns to expose the truth of those in the modern world: the good, the bad, and the ugly. Her inspiration primarily stems from life experiences, those who annoy her, ex-boyfriends, and the crazy dreams that pop into her head every once in a while.

The Broken Daughter

THE LOST DAUGHTERS TRILOGY BOOK TWO

VIOLA TEMPEST

www.ingramcontent.com/pod-product-compliance
Lightning Source LLC
Chambersburg PA
CBHW030145010826
48973CB00002B/735

9781959671176